Proof reading by Zelos
Cover Art by Orphan Print, Leominster

BOOKS IN THE DCS PALMER SERIES

BOOK 1. FUTURE RICHES

BOOK 2. THE FELT TIP MURDERS

BOOK 3. A KILLER IS CALLING

BOOK 4. POETIC JUSTICE

BOOK 5. LOOT

BOOK 6. I'M WITH THE BAND

BOOK 7. BURNING AMBITION

BOOK 8. TAKEAWAY TERROR

BOOK 9. MINISTRY OF MURDER

BOOK 10. THE BODY BUILDER

BOOK 11. SUCCESSION

BOOK 12. THE BLACK ROSE

BOOK 13. LAPTOPS CAN KILL

BEN NEVIS & THE GOLD DIGGER SERIES

BOOK 1. TURKISH DELIGHT
BOOK 2. NATIONAL TREASURE

FACTUAL BOOKS

LONDON CRIME An in-depth history of the major UK heists, gangs and geezers from 1930 until today including Brinks Matt, Great Train Robbery, Baker Street Bank, Hatton Garden and Knightsbridge Safe Deposit robberies, The Krays, The Richardsons, John Palmer, Jack Spot, Billy Hill, Bertie Smalls etc etc.. with new insights from the author's contacts.

UK SERIAL KILLERS 1030-20121. The lives, crimes and punishments of 44 UK Serial Killers from 1930 to present day. Includes Christie, Brady, The Wests, EWrskine, Bodkin,Bamber, Allitt, Tilley, Nilsen etc..

OTHERS

BIDDER BEWARE three light hearted tales about a dodgy UK auction house and the goings-on.

FRED KARNO biography of the UK's first impresario who took Charlie Chaplin and Stan Laurel to the USA and fame and fortune with his own life going from rags to riches and back to rags.

THE PALMER CASES BACKGROUND

Justin Palmer started off on the beat as a London policeman in the late 1970s and is now Detective Chief Superintendent Palmer, running the Metropolitan Police Force's Serial Murder Squad from New Scotland Yard. Not one to pull punches, or give a hoot for political correctness if it hinders his inquiries, Palmer has gone as far as he will go in the Met and knows it. Master of the one-line put down and a slave to his sciatica, he can be as nasty or as nice as he likes.

The mid 1990's was a time of re-awakening for Palmer, as the Information Technology revolution turned forensic science, communication and information-gathering skills upside down. Realising the value of this revolution to crime solving, Palmer co-opted Detective Sergeant Gheeta Singh into his team from the Yard's Cyber Crime unit. DS Singh has a degree in IT and was given the go ahead to update Palmer's department with all the computer hard and software she wanted; most of these she wrote herself, while some are, shall we say, of a grey area when it comes to privacy laws, data protection and accessing certain databases. Together with their civilian computer clerk called Claire they take on the serial killers of the UK.

On the personal front, Palmer has been married to his 'princess', or Mrs P. as she is known to everybody, for nearly thirty years. The romance blossomed after the young Detective Constable Palmer arrested most of her family, a bunch of South London petty criminals, in the 1960's. They have a nice house in the London suburb of Dulwich Village, and a faithful Springer called Daisy.

Gheeta Singh lives alone in a fourth floor Barbican apartment. Her parents arrived on these shores as a refugee family fleeing from Idi Amin's Uganda. Since then her father and brothers have built up a very successful computer parts supply company, in which it was assumed Gheeta would take an active role on graduating from University. She had other ideas on this, and also on the arranged marriage her mother and aunts still try to coerce her into. Gheeta has two loves, police work and technology, and thanks to Palmer she has her dream job.

The old copper's nose and gut feeling of Palmer, combined with the modern IT skills of DS Singh, makes them an unlikely but successful team. All their cases involve a serial killer, and twist and turn through red herrings and hidden clues, keeping the reader in suspense until the very end.

****

A KILLER IS CALLING

Chapter 1

'It's just a mess, Justin. An unholy fucking mess.'

Professor Latin held the brain scan negative up to the light box on the wall of the New Scotland Yard Pathology Lab and shook his head in bewilderment.

'Imagine a ball of rubber dropped onto a fucking hot stove, and this is what you would get; goo, sticky fucking goo.'

'Hmmm.'

Detective Chief Superintendent Palmer leant nearer to the light box as he fumbled his spectacles from the inside pocket of his trademark Prince of Wales check jacket and peered through them.

'So what causes this goo then? How does a human brain disintegrate into this kind of a mess?'

He looked at Latin inquisitively over the top of his specs, hoping for an answer that would at the very least give him some lead to pursue. He also hoped the answer would be without Professor Latin's liberal use of the *F* word, as his second-in-command Detective Sergeant Gheeta Singh was with them.

‘No idea, Justin, never come across it before. No fucking idea.’

Palmer’s hopes of an expletive-free answer sank without trace as the professor continued.

‘All I can tell you with certainty is that it’s not drugs. We’ve done a complete gas and TL chromatography screening, and nothing shows up. Fuck all.’

Behind them DS Gheeta Singh took a call on her mobile, catching Palmer’s eye as she spoke quietly into it. He raised his eyebrows to the heavens, anticipating problems as she clicked off, and her expression told him it was not good news.

‘What now?’ he said, slipping his specs back into his pocket.

‘I think we have another one, sir; he’s been riding the Circle line for a day, and nobody noticed.’

Detective Superintendent Justin Palmer loved his job and being one of the ‘old school’ detectives at the Yard, he treated his Serial Murder Squad like his own child. Now fast approaching retirement age and having turned down early retirement repeatedly each time it had been offered by the powers on the fifth floor, he was getting that buzz of excitement he always got as a new case unfolded. He knew that if he took an early retirement package, the first thing the suits on the fifth floor would do, would be to disband his squad and amalgamate it with the CID as a 'cost-cutting' exercise. As far as Palmer was concerned, that wasn't going to happen as long as he could put it off.

Outside the Pathology Laboratory he removed his grey trilby and settled into the back of a squad car, as Gheeta slipped in the other side. At least with the modern day squad cars he could stretch his legs a bit and relieve the stabs of sciatica that an old back problem had a habit of sending down his left thigh; the old style small Panda cars had been a source of continued pain, and he had been glad to see the back of them.

'Right then,' he said, nodding to the driver. 'Acton Tube station. Let's see what we have this time.'

****

The tube train had been backed off the District Line into the sidings at Acton Town station. Palmer and Singh stood in the carriage, looking at the body of a young man slumped on a corner seat. To all intents and purposes he could just have been asleep, resting against the heavy plastic partition beside his seat. But he was dead, not asleep. There were no immediately visible signs of why he was dead; just a thin line of congealed blood that ran from his left ear down over the lobe onto his neck.

The British Rail Police Inspector was unmoved; he'd seen it all before. The addicts seemed to find tube trains ideal for shooting up; he guessed it was because the trains all had a fairly quiet section to their routes once they were outside the hurly-burly of Westminster and the City. It was a section on the line where the lost souls of humanity could do the deed undisturbed. He had little doubt that the pathologist would find the tell-tale needle marks, and the dealers that rode the tube like parasites in a giant worm would now have one less customer to feed off.

'Usually vagrants or college kids; unusual to get one like this'

'Like this?'

Palmer was interested.

'Yes, a normal everyday-looking chap; smart dresser, too. His personal effects indicate he was a bank worker in the city, so odds on it's a Charlie OD. Usually is.'

'Maybe,' Palmer said. 'We will see once the autopsy is done.'

Sergeant Singh had noted Palmer's reluctance to say anything about the other three bodies already stored in the Wandsworth Police Morgue; three bodies that all had the same trace of blood from the ears. According to the pathology reports, none of them had been killed by a cocaine overdose, or indeed an overdose of anything.

'We've got officers going round to his work place and home now,' the BR Inspector continued.

Palmer was glad to hear that, as it meant he didn't have to spare any of his team to do it.

'Right. Keep me up to date, won't you please? My Sergeant will check in with you later for all the details; name, address, and so on.'

He squatted and looked carefully at the dead man's ear, before exchanging a knowing glance with Sergeant Singh.

****

Sitting in the back of the squad car travelling at less than walking pace in London's rush hour traffic wasn't Justin Palmer's favourite way of spending the afternoon, but it did give him a chance to recap on the case.

'So that's four now, Sergeant, and we've not got the faintest idea why any of them are dead. When do we get the biopsies back from the Maudsley?'

Professor Latin's Forensics team had taken mouth swabs and blood samples from each of the three previous victims and sent them over the Thames to the Tropical Diseases Laboratory at Maudsley Hospital in Camberwell. It was a long-shot, but you never knew; the victims may have had contact with a friend, or a friend of a friend returning from the tropics with a virus.

'They should be back tomorrow, guv; so they said, anyway. Can't be a disease though, can it?'

Well, if it is – and it's catching – we've probably got it. Not a very nice thought, eh?'

He shifted uneasily in his seat.

'No, not very nice thought at all. Thanks for sharing that, guv.'

'But,' Palmer said, giving her a reassuring smile. 'Three victims in five weeks, and none related to each other by family or work; doesn't point to a nasty little bug flying around does it, eh? And their nearest and dearest would be dropping like flies as well by now if it was, and they haven't. But there has to be a connection between them somewhere; there always is.'

He sighed loudly and settled back in his seat.

'I wouldn't mind a nice little bug to wipe out some of this traffic right now. I thought this congestion charging fiasco was going to clear the London streets and get the traffic moving?'

The driver gave a sarcastic laugh.

'Ha! It cleared off the Mayor's budget deficit, Chief; that's all it did. Traffic's just as bad, if not worse.'

Palmer smiled.

'Ah yes, but I bet it also gave our wonderful Mayor a pot of cash so he can keep the rates down and get re-elected. Never take a politician at face value, Constable.'

'I never thought of it that way, sir,' the driver said, nodding as it sank in. 'The crafty bugger.' 'You can bet the Mayor thought of it that way.'

Palmer learnt a long, long time ago that nobody in public life ever did anything for the public good, only for their *own* good.

DS Singh smiled. Palmer's sarcasm amused her; he had a way of making people look at things differently. He'd impressed on her a long time ago to never take anything at face value, that there was nearly always an ulterior motive behind the face. Or maybe he was just a grumpy old man.

She checked the emails on her laptop as they came to another halt in the traffic in the Strand. Nothing important, just her auntie asking if she'd spoken to *'that nice young Indian businessman whose telephone number I gave you'*.... Soon, very soon, Gheeta would have to have an almighty row with her auntie and her mum about arranged marriages. She grimaced at the thought of it. Generation gaps, culture clashes – the world had changed so much in the last few decades that some of the older generation were having trouble keeping pace with it, mum and auntie being two of them. She turned her mind back to the case.

'You want to get a team meeting on this one, guv?'

'No, not yet,' he said, thinking for a moment. 'I'm not really sure which way to go with this case as yet. Just keep putting all the information on the victims into the computer programmes as it comes in and see if we can get any matches.'

****

Chapter 2

Several of the hierarchy at New Scotland Yard had raised worried frowns when Palmer had plucked novice WPC Gheeta Singh from the West Central street beat and given her half his operational budget and a free hand to bring in computers to his Serial Murder Squad office. But Palmer was a wily old fox, and forty-plus years in the Met had honed his ability to pick out winners early on. He'd first been impressed with WPC Singh's IT aptitudes when she was able to re-programme his crashed HOLMES database terminal in half an hour, a job the outside contractors usually had two people working on for three days at six hundred quid a day; at that time he didn't know Gheeta Singh was a university graduate in IT and Computing, or that she privately considered the Yard's systems to be very outdated and vulnerable.

Her parents had brought the family into the UK, fleeing Idi Amin's Uganda, and had set up a technology business now run by her three elder brothers. Her father had steered her education through technical college and university, grooming her to take a lead role in the family business; but Gheeta's heart was set on police work from an early age, and there it was to stay. When Palmer had seconded her to his unit for a three-month trial and let her range free over all the systems in his team room, she was in her element; upgrading, creating shortcuts, rewriting and deleting programmes, adding new ones, and generally kicking the systems into the 21st century. After just one month Palmer pulled the necessary strings, and the move was made permanent.

That was four years ago; Singh was now a Detective Sergeant, and Palmer knew she was the obvious one to take his role when he finally succumbed to retirement in a year's time. Well, Mrs P. thought it was to be in a year's time, but Palmer had no intention at all of hanging up his brain and becoming an assistant gardener to Mrs P. in one year's time, or in five years' time come to that. No, retirement was not a pleasing thought to him. Mrs P. ran the house and garden with military precision, and he generally felt he was in the way if he took so much as a day off work, and usually spent most of it finding excuses to go out; and even his faithful dog Daisy drew the line at being dragged out for *five* walks a day, even though she was a Springer with all the excess energy of that breed.

At New Scotland Yard they signed in and climbed the stairs to the fourth-floor offices which housed the Serial Murder Squad and went straight into the team room. This was a large open-space room with all Singh's computers and terminals along one side on a work surface, and various tables and chairs scattered around the rest of the room like a wedding party aftermath. It used to be the old canteen before the modernisation of the Yard, and every time he came into the room Palmer always got the well-remembered whiff of early morning bacon sandwiches that had permeated the walls over the years; too many early morning bacon sandwiches, according to Mrs P., who worried about his expanding waistline. He removed his trilby and jacket and slung them on a handy table next to where his civilian operator was working a terminal.

'Claire, are you still here? Your hubby won't be pleased.'

Sergeant Singh had first met Claire in the admin typing pool and done a 'Palmer' on her, having her transferred as administration clerk to the team after noticing her reading Computer Weekly on her lunch break rather than the usual Hello or Nuts magazine; a chat over coffee had yielded the information that Claire was doing an evening IT course, and was also something of a computer 'nerd'. She turned to greet them as they entered.

‘Yep, still here I’m afraid sir; married to my job.’

‘Very commendable, but I don’t think your old man will appreciate it. Can’t have the Yard cited in divorce papers.’

Gheeta unloaded her laptop from her shoulder and sat on the chair next to Claire.

‘Anything?’

‘No, nothing at all. I can’t understand it – all we’ve got that ties the victims together is the way they died, those blood trickles from the ear. It’s like somebody just picked them out at random and zapped them with something.’

‘Could well be that’s exactly what happened,’ Palmer said. ‘Random killings. Our killer gets up in the morning and has the urge to murder, so out he goes and kills the first unsuspecting poor blighter he can without being seen. An empty tube train carriage is ideal – he does the job and hops off at the next station; anybody getting on the carriage would think our victim was just sleeping. Is the final pathology report through yet?’

Claire shook her head.

‘No, sir. I’ll chase it in the morning.’

Gheeta sensed a lilt to Palmer’s question.

'What's your interest in that report, guv? You've an idea, haven't you? I can tell. What are you expecting it to say?'

'Nothing really,' Palmer said. He sat and tipped a chair back against the wall as his feet clattered up onto a table. 'But for blood to run there has to be a wound, so I just thought they might find a needle hole or something inside the ear.'

Singh nodded.

'Yes, but it's not very likely that the victims would allow somebody to push a hypodermic in their ear, is it guv? Not going to sit there and say "carry on old chap, help yourself", are they?'

'Not very likely at all – *if* they knew it was being done, Sergeant. But what about if they *didn't* know it was being done?'

'How do you mean?'

'Well, maybe the killer chloroformed them first. Just an idea.'

He swung his feet down, got up and crossed the room to stand in front of the case progress board on the wall. Across one wall of the team room Palmer had a wide plug board for updating the crime trail as it unwound; an *aide memoir* that he could ponder like a grand master ponders over a chessboard before making the next move. The three victims' pictures and crime scene photos were all that graced it at present. Palmer pointed his finger at the first victim's set of photos.

'Hannah Robson, nondescript housewife, 32 years old; just done the weekly shop and then drops dead in the front seat of her car in Asda's car park. A busy car park, so we can assume that if she were attacked in any way she'd have shouted, and it would have been noticed. Not a weak lady, far from it – in fact, just come from her twice weekly gym work out. Very capable of defending herself if need be. But, looking at it from another way, she's just come from the gym; she's tired, and now she's done the weekly shopping as well, so she slumps into the car and – don't forget it was a very hot day – she takes a nap.'

'And Mr X – the killer – comes up with his needle and injects?'

Gheeta wasn't convinced.

'Could have, why not?'

He pointed to the second set of pictures.

'Victim number two: Samuel Haines, schoolboy, sixteen; getting his books together in his room at 7.30 in the morning, and then, when mum goes to hurry him up, there he is – dead.'

'So where did the killer come from?'

'With Samuel, I don't know,' Palmer admitted, shaking his head. 'I just have no idea. But with Arthur-'

Palmer moved to the third victim's pictures.

'With Arthur, I do. Arthur McGann was in a late night launderette; bachelor boy Arthur is doing his own wash, eleven at night. Round and round goes the tub; Arthur is sleepy and dozes off.'

'Enter the killer.'

'Yes.'

Palmer swung round and faced them, putting his hands in his pockets.

'And the same with our chap on the tube train. He just dozed off; see it all the time on the tube.'

'And the killer injected him in the ear without waking him? What about the other passengers?'

'We don't know that there were any. If the killer is out looking for a victim, he's going to be in no hurry and wait his chance – after all, any victim will do. All he has to do is bide his time until fate presents him with one, which it did. So the answer to your original question about my interest in the Pathology Lab report is really twofold: are there any puncture marks inside the ears of the victims; and, if so, is there a foreign substance in that *goo*, as Professor Latin calls it, that used to be their brains?'

'That *fucking* goo, guv.'

Singh did a passable Professor Latin impression, highlighting the swear word.

'Been to see the professor, eh?' Claire laughed. 'Do you think his language is as bad when he's at home? I can't see his wife standing for that.'

'She's worse than him,' Palmer said, being the only one to have met her. 'East End girl, and you know what their language is like.'

Claire smiled at the inference; Gheeta lived in the East End.

'What did he think was the cause of death?'

Singh shrugged.

'He didn't know.'

'Bit sinister isn't it,' Claire said, with a shiver.

'It seems that way at the moment Claire,' Gheeta sighed. 'But it'll come together, it always does.'

Palmer smiled, hearing Sergeant Singh using one of his own phrases.

'Sergeant, you get more like me with every case. You'll develop sciatica next.'

'Cynicism more likely,' said Claire.

Palmer chuckled.

'Copper's stock in trade, Claire: cynicism, sciatica and optimism. They go hand-in-hand with the job. And divorces too, so you get off home, young lady; you've done quite enough for today.'

Sergeant Singh walked over and joined Palmer at the wall board.

'Be nice to have a murder weapon wouldn't it, guv? Even a bullet or a knife wound – just something to get working on. Got nothing yet, have we? If Pathology come up with no pin holes and no substance, we've even less than nothing.'

Palmer nodded in agreement.

'We've got to find the link, Sergeant, that little thread; that common denominator that ties all these unfortunate people together. Somewhere there is a link – as always, we've just got to find it. More than likely it's staring us in the face right now; we can't see it for looking, but it's there, I'd bet my pension on it. It's in there somewhere… but where?'

****

Chapter 3

'Not a sausage.'

Sergeant Singh ripped the fax off the machine. It was the following morning. Palmer looked up from the mountain of papers on his desk.

'What do you mean, "not a sausage"? I don't want a sausage, I want a pinhole or a substance!'

'No pinhole no substance – just nothing, guv,' she said as she placed the Pathology Lab report in front of him. 'Zilch.'

Palmer scanned the paper for a minute and wasn't happy. He read aloud from the report.

'*Undetermined intrusion*, what does that mean then? We don't pay those lab boys to come up with nothing. *The disintegration of the lower left part of the brain in each victim was caused by an undetermined intrusion* – in other words, they haven't a clue. Great, very helpful.'

He put the report down on his desk with the other papers.

'If there's nothing there to be found, guv, they won't find anything.'

'Yes, I suppose that's true,' Palmer acquiesced. 'Any joy on Joe Public in the tube train?'

'Mr James Fennel, guv. Clean as a whistle, bright upstanding member of his local community, leaves a grieving mother and father and a vacancy at Lloyds Bank city branch.'

Palmer sighed loudly.

'This isn't good is it, eh? Four bodies all killed the same way, and no motive or weapon. I'm beginning to believe in aliens now.'

'The truth is out there somewhere, guv. Just got to find it.'

Singh turned on her heels and made for the door.

'Some old copper I used to know was always saying that. Then he went off his head and started believing in aliens.'

She was out the door before Palmer's hurriedly aimed biro hit it behind her.

In the team room, Claire was pinning up the James Fennel crime scene pictures as Sergeant Singh walked in.

'Good looking lad, wasn't he?'

Singh stood beside her and gazed at the slumped body in the picture.

'Just looks asleep really. If you were on the train you wouldn't know he was dead, would you? No wonder he was going round and round the Circle line all day. Did you get a copy of the Pathology report?'

'Yes, disappointing eh? Complete blank. Bet the governor was overjoyed at that.'

'He wasn't best pleased.'

The door opened quickly and Palmer stood there, hurriedly putting on his coat; the glint in his eye was strong, the smile was back.

'Get your laptop, Sergeant; we have lift-off. Some nutter has just phoned the Mayor's office and demanded a million quid or he'll kill a thousand people.'

Sergeant Singh slung the laptop strap over her shoulder and joined him.

'Is there a connection?'

'Oh yes, he knew the locations of all four of our victims.'

Palmer was smiling broadly now.

'Game on.'

****

The Mayor was not too bothered and carried on working through a stack of official papers with his secretary, who was trying hard to appear unflustered as Palmer and Singh waited in his office for the Mayor's IT department man to search through the telephone recording machine to find the right call and replay it. The PR man fumbled with the buttons on his jacket, trying to think of way to spin all this to the

Mayor's advantage if it went pear-shaped. He fidgeted nervously as the in-house techie pressed the buttons on the machine, trying to extract the ransom call from the other 3000 of the day.

'Is this going to take all day?'

The Mayor was getting impatient. A rather obese man with a shock of red hair, his political career had languished in the doldrums until a surprise win in the Mayoral elections had elevated him to this important position; a position with salary, expenses and a pension that he wished to keep, and with an election coming up soon the last thing he wanted was some idiot wasting his time with a false ransom demand. So far all his promises about cutting London traffic, clearing the beggars off the streets and improving the public transport had come to nothing, and the only success he could claim was ridding Trafalgar Square of pigeons; and all they'd done was to fly up the road to Piccadilly Circus and crap all over Eros instead. He hadn't formulated a final manifesto for the upcoming election yet, although he knew he wanted to cut the household rates bill, which was a surefire winner; but which unsuspecting department was going to have their budget plundered to pay for it, and how could he placate them? Probably have to promise some civil servant an MBE in the next honours list; the PM would push that through if it meant keeping the London mayoral seat within the party.

The techie was having problems isolating the ransom call and was looking for an excuse.

'There are 4000 calls a day on this machine, and I've got find and then isolate your one from that lot, mate. Not easy.'

He pressed a button and a number showed on the LED display. The voice of Mrs Randels of 23 Peach Crescent, Brixton came through the speaker, enquiring about waste collection after a bank holiday. Sergeant Singh leant past him.

'Wrong sequence – here, let me have a go. We have the same machines at the Yard.'

She pressed the right buttons in the right orde,r and the LED showed a flying decrease to '0'. 'Press the forward arrow when you're ready,' she said, smiling at him and stepping back.

The Mayor, not known for mincing his words or for his diplomatic skills, raised his eyes from the papers he was studying to the technician.

'I suppose you're somebody's son or nephew, are you? Obviously you didn't get the job on ability.'

He shifted his gaze to Palmer.

'You ready to hear it then, Justin?'

He was interrupted as his mobile rang on his desk.

'Shit,' he said as he answered the call. 'Yes? Okay… but I'm busy now for about twenty minutes so get them coffees and take them on a tour of the building or something, all right? I'll be as quick as I can.'

He clicked the mobile off and put it on top of his papers.

'Bloody union officials, they think they can wander in and you'll drop everything for them. Sorry Justin, where were we… oh yes, are you ready to listen?'

Palmer smiled.

'Thank you, Mr Mayor, I think so.'

He raised an enquiring eyebrow to Sergeant Singh, who had taken a lead from her laptop and interfaced it through a digital recorder box and stuck a small listening microphone next to the machine, so that she would get a perfect digital copy of the call downloaded to her computer. She nodded to the technician, whose face was still a bright shade of red from the Mayor's comment, and he pressed the button. They heard the operator take the call.

'Good afternoon, London Mayor's Office – how can I help you?'

An obviously distorted voice came from the speaker, sounding like a Dalek.

'Do you record these calls?'

'We do, sir, yes.'

'Good. I've killed four people: a lady in the car park at Southfields, a boy in his home in Harrow, a man in the launderette at Acton, and one more on a tube train. All have a wound within an ear. I intend to kill one thousand more unless I get ten million pounds. I will ring you again in four days time at the same time with a little demonstration. Goodbye.'

The caller rang off.

'Hello? Hello?' the operator said, trying to reconnect.

The recording clicked off. Singh unplugged her leads and pushed them into her bag. The Mayor chucked his glasses on his papers and leaned back in his over-large leather chair, rubbing his eyes.

'Well, Justin, what have I got – a harmless idiot, or a potential mass murderer?'

Palmer shrugged his shoulders.

'Well sir, hard to say for sure – but whoever that was certainly knows more about the four murders than he would do if he wasn't involved.'

'Could have got all that information from the newspapers, couldn't he?'

'Most of it, yes sir. But the tube train murder hasn't been released to the press yet, nor the information about their ears having similar wounds. He couldn't know about that.'

'That is a bit worrying. So what do we do now then? Can't pay him, out of the question – pay one and there'd be a queue from here to Lands End.'

'Sit tight for the time being, sir; that's all we can do at present, I'm afraid. We'll get a trace on the call and hope the chap's not covered his tracks too well.'

Sergeant Singh looked up from her laptop screen.

'It's a mobile, sir. Not much chance of a trace result there.'

The Mayor was confused.

'Why not? Mobiles have numbers and are registered, aren't they? This one is.'

He waved a hand at his own mobile phone on the desk.

Singh smiled nicely as she explained.

'You don't *have* to register a mobile, sir. Just buy it, put in a SIM card, and away you go; if it's a pre-paid voucher phone you can buy call minutes at any supermarket or corner shop. We can get the number of the phone without any trouble and trace the call back to it and find the area where the call was made; but who owns it, and where it is now – that is another matter.'

'Probably at the bottom of the Thames by now, I shouldn't wonder,' added Palmer. 'Or had its memory wiped clean, another SIM card popped in, and hey presto – a new phone with a new number, in which case it's totally untraceable.'

'Okay, so what about his little *demonstration* in four days' time? I don't like the sound of that.'

'No,' Palmer said with a frown. 'Nor do I. Let's hope we get to him by then.'

****

Chapter 4

Sergeant Singh lay wide awake in her fifth-floor Barbican apartment, looking across the bedroom and out of the panoramic window to the dark sky above, where a few dark clouds reflected the orange red lights of the city back to their source. She shifted her legs in the bed as her mind pondered the day's work. They really had nothing to go on; just the phone call to the Mayor's office, and she felt sure that wouldn't yield much.

A kiss on her shoulder made her aware that Mark, her partner for the last 6 months, was stirring beside her.

****

It was a long time since Palmer had had a kiss on his shoulder; these days, after thirty-eight-plus years of marriage he was lucky to get a peck on the cheek when he left for work in the morning. It wasn't morning, but was very late night as Palmer stood looking out of his bedroom window, past his back garden and over the trees and grass of Dulwich Park. Everything seemed coated in a blue hue from the moonlight falling from the clear night sky, but he could see dark clouds forming in the distance.

Behind him in the king-size double bed, Mrs P. slept soundly. The luminous hands of his bedside alarm said two ten. She would have been asleep since eleven; creature of habit was Mrs P., and eleven was bedtime, come hell or high water. Palmer had once tried to work out the number of times in a year that he actually got to bed at the same time as her, but after he got to three months and had only made it add up to five days, he gave up. Thirty-eight years married to a copper was a long time, and he fully appreciated the sacrifices Mrs P. had made with the words '*I do'*. He often wondered whether she had regretted it.

Oh well, three children and eight grandchildren kept her life full, while serial murders with no clues kept *his* life full. But now the adrenalin was flowing; this latest killer had broken cover with his phone call. Yes, he thought, the game was now on. He unintentionally said it out loud as he made for his side of the bed.

'Game on.'

'Oh no it isn't, not tonight Justin,' said Mrs P., who was still just about awake. 'I've got a WI coffee morning tomorrow and I need my sleep, so behave yourself. Anyway, you know it sets your sciatica off. Night-night sweetheart.'

****

Chapter 5

'What sort of demonstration?'

Claire typed away as she asked Sergeant Singh the question. It was the next morning and Singh stood coffee in hand at the wall board, hoping for divine guidance to give her a lead.

'I don't know, Claire, I wish I did. But it's got to be another murder, hasn't it? Just to prove he can do it – to prove he has the power.'

Claire stopped typing and swung her seat round.

'God, that's some sort of challenge to the boss, isn't it? *I'm going to murder somebody on such and such date – stop me if you can.* Bit of a heavy scene.'

'Yes, very heavy – and not much we can do to stop him at the moment.'

Singh walked to the work surfaces that ranged along one wall, and where four state of the art computers were sifting and sorting every little detail they could find on the victims. She patted one lovingly as though it was a pet.

'Come on you little darling, spill out a match; in fact, spill out anything.'

Sergeant Singh had worked all the hours God gave her for six months when Palmer had passed her his office budget, and told her rather bluntly: 'Get what you need, do what you want to do, but make it work.' She'd taken the basics of every computer matching programme – from Find Your Perfect Partner to the Formula One racing optimum fuel mix programmes – ripped them apart and rebuilt them on top of the rather tired police-issue HOLMES programme software. They were programmed to look and find the slightest match between subjects, and everything was printed out; if two victims had the same tooth capped, it would pick it up; but more usefully it picked up when they had the same friend, or same tastes in food, or had been to the same primary school, or… well, just about anything that Palmer could send his team out to probe and prod, in the hope that underneath that insignificant morsel was the key that he was looking for to break a case open.

The success rate had stunned Palmer. Not one to fight shy of new technology, he had prayed it would come up with the goods on a couple of seemingly hopeless dead end case,s so that he could justify his spending to the suits on the fifth floor; more than that would be a big bonus. Not only did he get more – much more – but the side effects were enormous. The case solve time was cut by seventy percent, and the clear-up rate for his department since the computers came in was a perfect one hundred percent. The flip side, of course, was that along with the plaudits came the extra workload.

Palmer was an old style copper who solved crimes, and it was just fate that as a young detective he was put on a couple of serial murder cases that were going nowhere and had cracked them; in so doing he got himself a reputation for the genre, and now every unsolved serial murder in the UK landed on his desk, usually after local CID units had finished with them when they were as cold as ice.

Claire sighed as she checked the computers findings.

'Nothing coming out, except that James Fennel…'

Singh moved over behind her.

'The tube train guy?'

'Yes. He had his mobile phone stolen.'

'I've had two pinched myself. Big business now, usually two youngsters on a moped.'

'Yes, but he had his stolen on the tube.'

'How do you know that?'

'Because I ran all the victims through the mobile phone registered users databases to see if we could get a record of any of them phoning each other.'

The printer beside her computer started to whir out papers.

'And?'

'Here, I've printed it out. Look.'

Claire ripped the paper from the printer and laid it on the desk in front of them.

'They all had mobiles, and none have made any calls since their murders – which is what you would expect, of course. All except Fennel's; his mobile went mad on international calls for a period of six hours after the time of his murder, then the credits ran out and it went silent.'

'Usual scam then, eh?' Gheeta said. 'Nick the phone and hammer it until you get cut off or run out of credits, then slip in a new SIM card and flog it with a new number. Easy money.'

She picked up the print out.

'I'll see if the governor wants anything done with this. I bet he will; probably have me tracing all the calls. Still, you never know – if the killer took it I don't think he would be so daft as to phone home, but you never know...'

****

Sergeant Singh was right; Palmer had her trace every call made on the Fennel mobile. They all terminated in India or the Caribbean, which underlined her assumption that some opportunist phone thief had probably seen Fennel slumped in the corner seat of the tube and, thinking he was asleep, had stolen the mobile. Obviously being a professional thief he would have had it, and any others he'd managed to steal, into a back street phone shop within hours, and been charging half the normal cost for overseas calls to customers who weren't bothered about the phone's history, just the half price calls. All the calls made prior to those checked out as Fennel's family or work numbers.

****

Chapter 6

The Mayor wasn't very happy. The four days were up, and Palmer's team had taken over his office in anticipation that this serial killer would keep his word and phone. He really didn't need this; he was desperately trying to think up some scam to have the public praise him and landslide him back into office, and now he'd got an idiot killing his electors and demanding ten million to stop.

'I thought you would have nailed him by now, Justin.'

Palmer smiled a '*you do your job, and I'll do mine'* type smile.

'Not a lot to go on, Mr Mayor. Random killers hold all the cards 'til they make a mistake.'

The voice print analysis had come back negative; it didn't match any others on file. The recording had been put through the machines and the distortion taken out, to give the caller's real voice as far as possible, and then sent for profile analysis. It came back as London, educated male; and that was about the extent of the profiler's report. Palmer had remarked sarcastically how useful that was, as it cut the suspect list to about 7 million.

Technology he could see the benefits of; psychoanalytic profiling he couldn't.

He looked round the Mayor's office, which now resembled the inside of GCHQ at Cheltenham: banks of terminals, high-speed tracing equipment, direct lines to phone number data banks, and several of the Met's technicians that Sergeant Singh had pulled in for the operation; Singh was doing a last minute check on the phone amplifiers. All was ready – if the killer called, they'd have a fix on his position within 80 seconds; which might be totally useless because ransom-type phone calls usually come from unregistered mobiles, or public pay phones in busy pedestrian areas that a patrol car couldn't get to fast. Railway stations, shopping malls, airport concourses and the like were usually favoured.

The Mayor strummed his fingers on the desk and tried to look unworried by the whole affair. His secretary fumbled nervously with her blouse collar, and the PR man was thinking that the best way out this – if it did all go wrong – was for the Mayor to make a point to the press about his faith in the police and confidence in their methods, thus subtly passing the buck from his desk to theirs

The Mayor stretched his arms above his head and sighed.

'Looks like Microsoft's head office in here, eh? Hope the bastard phones after all this trouble.'

Palmer was confident.

'He'll phone alright, sir; I'll put my mortgage on it. This one is a very clever sod, I'm afraid. He's got everything planned out, and so far his plan is working well for him.'

The loud ringing of the desk phone amplified through the speakers cut through the room. Everybody stiffened. Singh put her hand by the receiver, ready to lift it for the telephonist to take the call. She looked at the telephonist, who was quite pale.

'You all right?'

'Yes, I'll be fine.'

'Okay, just be normal – like taking any other call.'

She looked to Palmer, who nodded. She raised the receiver for the telephonist, who then took it.

'Mayor's Office, how may I help you?'

The unmistakeable distorted voice came over the speakers, loud and menacing.

'I know you are surrounded by police, and I know they are tracing this call. So you have precisely four seconds to put the Mayor on the line before I ring off. One...'

Singh look anxiously at Palmer, while around the room technicians were flicking switches and hitting keypads in the race to pinpoint the call.

'...two...'

Singh held up four fingers to Palmer and mouthed: 'Four seconds not enough time.'

Palmer nodded. He looked to the Mayor and mouthed: 'Keep him talking.' The Mayor nodded and stepped towards the telephonist.

'...three...'

The Mayor took the phone on Palmer's signal.

'This is the Mayor speaking. Who are you, and what do you want?'

There was nail-biting silence, and Palmer wondered whether the line had dropped out and they had lost him. Then the speakers gave forth again with the Dalek voice.

'Have ten million pounds ready to be switched into a foreign bank account by this time in four days.'

The Mayor tried to interrupt, but the voice carried on regardless. Singh looked at Palmer.

'It's a pre-recorded message, sir. Tape probably.'

The voice continued as Palmer nodded that he understood.

'Should that money not be in the account within twenty-four hours of you being given its location and number, then at least one thousand people will die – one thousand people at least...'

The voice paused for effect.

'And now for the demonstration I promised you... I will count to ten. One... two...three...'

Proceedings were briefly interrupted as the Mayor's mobile rang on his desk. The Mayor waved a hand to his secretary to take the call. She picked it up and whispered: 'Hello?'

It was the last word she ever spoke. Silently, like a ship slowly sinking beneath the waves, she dropped to the floor, the mobile spilling from her hand and sliding away. The distorted voice counted on as Palmer and Singh reached her. He checked her pulse as Singh started CPR; nothing, no heart beat. Singh moved the secretary's head face up to start mouth to mouth. They both spotted it at the same time and stopped in their tracks. It wasn't much, but there it was – a tiny scarlet, glistening trickle of blood running from her ear. The Mayor was at his office door, shouting down the corridor for medics. The voice on the speaker carried on.

'*...eight...nine... ten... I think I have made my point by now, haven't I? Ten million ready, in four days' time.*'

The phone clicked off, leaving a hum from the speakers. Palmer crossed quickly to the technicians.

'Get anything?'

One of them shook his head.

'Nothing, sir; no fix. He's a clever sod – routed it through ISDN internet lines and proxy servers.'

Palmer looked to Sergeant Singh for a translation, although he knew what she would tell him; but she was still trying to get life back into the secretary. Handing the CPR over to the newly arrived medics, she got up and crossed over to him.

'Basically sir, he's got the recording set up somewhere on a timer, and set it to ring this number using an internet modem connection; which means he can program the call to go through lots of different servers before it gets here. Sort of a scenic round-the-houses route, so to speak.'

'Can we still trace it back to the source?'

'We can try, but my bet is he's using proxy servers – the sort of places you go to get an encrypted pseudonym and be untraceable, if you wanted to surf the kiddy porn sites and not be found out. They're big business now, and mostly sited in Russia and Eastern Europe; unlicensed and unaccountable. If he's routed the call through three or four of them, forget it. We'll never trace him.'

The paramedics tried in vain to revive the Mayor's secretary, and after a while they shook their heads, covered her over with a blanket, and took her away on a stretcher. The pathologist was called. The Mayor sat back at his desk, visibly shaken and silent for once. He reached down to retrieve his mobile. Palmer's strong hand caught his wrist and stopped him.

'Sorry Mayor, we'll need that. We may have better luck tracing that call than we have with the other one.'

'He meant to kill me, Justin,' the Mayor said quietly. 'I'd normally have taken that call. It should be me under the blanket. Jesus!'

'Well, if we don't get lucky soon you might need another hundred thousand blankets.'

The Mayor took in the gravity of the situation.

'I'll pay the little shit.'

'And when he comes back for more will you pay him again? And maybe again after that?' Palmer spoke sense, and the Mayor knew it.

'Okay, I'll pay him the first lot and you can follow the money and get him that way. It should be easy enough to trace through bank to bank account transfers.'

'Easy enough over here sir, yes. But what if the bank he transfers it to is Swiss? Took the victims of the Nazis sixty years to even get an acknowledgement their stolen money was in a Swiss bank, let alone get it back. Lots of safe havens in the world for illicit money if you've enough of it, and I think ten million is more than enough.'

'So what do we do?'

'We hope four days is enough time for us to dig out a lead on the bastard and close in, that's what we do, sir. And at least we know we're not looking for a hypodermic needle anymore.'

'Sir.'

Sergeant Singh caught his attention. He joined her and the technicians who were engrossed looking at a green monitor screen on which a series of zigzags moved up and down the tail, zagging to join the head and repeat the move.

‘Pretty patterns, eh?’

The screen meant nothing to Palmer.

‘It’s called a ‘mouse trap’, sir,’ Gheeta explained. ‘Our killer certainly knows what he’s doing. The call was routed through proxy servers in Eastern Europe and Indonesia, and then routed back on itself. Once the call was terminated it’s like a hall of mirrors – each trace just sends you back to the last one, and you basically go around in circles retracing your steps time and time again. It’s a favourite ploy of some internet web sites so you can’t leave them; only way to bust it is to turn off. Do that and you lose the whole thing.’

‘Is there any way we can get to the original source of the call?’

‘No sir, no way.’

****

Chapter 7

The high panelled corridor of the Defence Ministry echoed Palmer and Singh's footsteps as they followed their uniformed escort who strode quickly along it. Palmer had no idea why Assistant Commissioner Bateman had called him urgently up to the fifth floor at the Yard and told him he was to go over to the Defence Ministry immediately for a meeting with Lt Commander Layne. Their escort paused outside a door marked NAVY PRIVATE. His loud knock was answered by a muffled '*enter*' from within.

Inside Lt Cmmdr Harry Layne rose from behind his enormous boardroom desk. With hand outstretched, he beamed at Palmer as they entered.

'Justin you old fox, how are you? How's the lovely Mrs P., eh? Still wasting her life on you?'

'Hello Harry, we are both fine thank you. And your lot?'

'Yes, all okay thanks. Offspring all fled the nest now of course, same as yours. Sit down, sit down.'

Palmer introduced Sergeant Singh, who was never really surprised at Palmer's contacts. He seemed to be able to produce somebody who knew somebody who could help whenever they floated into new uncharted waters. The Commander smiled at Singh and motioned them both towards large comfy chairs, then retook his seat behind the desk before offering an explanation.

'Justin, or should I say DCS Palmer and I both started our respective careers about the same time, Sergeant; and at every damn management course I went on there he was, usually disrupting them by asking sensible questions which of course you mustn't do, ha-ha.'

He giggled like a child at the memory.

'We had some damn good times, didn't we Justin? Damn good times. Didn't do one stick of good for our management skills, but certainly honed our pontoon and drinking skills!'

Palmer gave an embarrassed smile. Day one of his '*four days*' given by the killer was coming to its end and he wanted to get on, not chat about old times. The Commander must have learned something from one of their courses, as he picked up the serious vibes from Palmer and settled down to serious work. He thrust sheets of paper over the desk to each of them.

'Sign those, please.'

Palmer took out his pen.

'Official Secrets Act?'

'Yes, the information you want is embargoed I'm afraid.'

Singh followed Palmer's lead and turned to the last page and signed it. It was obviously just a usual formality, although her curiosity would have liked her to read the whole thing; all fourteen pages of it.

The Commander reached over and took the papers back, countersigned them and put them in a drawer under his desk.

'Right, that's out of the way; so now you can bring me up to speed. What have you got so far then on this killer who's holding the Mayor to ransom?'

Between them Palmer and Singh went through the case, from the beginning to the unfortunate incident in the Mayor's office. When they had finished the Commander sat back with a long sigh.

'The man you're looking for is George North.'

Both Palmer and Singh were a trifle stunned by this. Both thought it prudent to stay silent and await the explanation for such a direct statement.

'I want to bring in one of our security people to give you information on North and work with you on the case; he knows North inside and out. Any objections, Justin?'

Palmer shrugged.

'No, we could certainly use some help on this one.'

The commander pressed his desk intercom.

'Would you come in now please.'

He took two large photos from his desk and passed one each to Singh and Palmer.

'That is George North.'

The photos showed a uniformed naval officer, late middle-age and serious looking.

A side door to the room opened quietly to admit a young man, also in Naval Officer uniform, who crossed silently to the desk and stood beside Layne. Only when she looked up from the photo towards him did Sergeant Singh's heart miss a beat. The young officer was her partner, Mark. They looked at each other. Neither the Commander nor Palmer, who was committing George North's face to his memory, noticed the sign of recognition on her face. Layne did the introductions.

'This is Mark Randall, he's handling this case from our end. Mark, this is Detective Sergeant Singh and Detective Chief Superintendent Palmer, Serial Murder Squad, New Scotland Yard.'

They nodded to each other and smiled the perfunctory smile as Randall sat down in a chair alongside them. Palmer guessed he was MI6. The Commander ran over the brief details of the murders for him.

'Looks like we have the proverbial 'loose cannon' out there, eh?'

Randall nodded.

'What he has in his armoury is far more dangerous than any cannon,' he added. 'George North is, or was, one of Portland Down's top boffins; he was seconded there from AT&T research twelve years ago. At AT&T he was team leader, researching wavelength possibilities on very high ultra frequency radio bands for communications; he was years ahead of anybody else in his field, and he knew it. He came to us and said that the research he had completed had convinced him that he could make a people destructive weapon with NCD, no collateral damage; in other words, he could kill an enemy inside buildings or vehicles without damage to that building or vehicle using a wavelength frequency signal. Now, replace the word vehicle with the word submarine or even aircraft carrier, and you can see the ramifications of what he was claiming. Taking it to the maximum, it would mean de-populating a big city whilst doing no structural damage, leaving the infrastructure and means of government intact.'

'By '*de-populating*' you mean killing the population?'

Singh looked him straight in the eyes, having regained her inner composure

'Yes, I do.'

Palmer was having difficulty with the concept before him

'This is science fiction, isn't it? My God.'

'Science fiction has a habit of becoming fact over time, sir,' Randall said seriously. 'North was only on the very first tentative experiments using UHF sound; but his results were promising, and he had an increase in funding and staff. He had found the wave band and pitch that could render the recipient inoperative.'

'You mean dead?' Singh said. Their eyes met again. Hers were cold.

'Yes Sergeant, dead.'

Palmer shifted in his chair.

'You mean that North had actually tested this bloody thing on humans and killed them?'

'I don't have that information, sir.'

'Yes you do.'

Palmer wanted the facts; he wanted to know what sort of weapon they were dealing with. Randall remained silent, until the Commander came to his rescue.

'If it was tested, Justin, it would have been tested in the field; in a war theatre like Iraq, or Syria.'

'I didn't think you'd pop down Morrison's and zap the bacon counter, Harry. So what happened? Why did George North go off the rails?'

'Well,' Randall carried on. 'It's important to say at this point that North is not running around with a weapon of mass destruction that he can point at a building and kill everybody inside with. He does have the capability of killing by subjecting a person to the frequency, but that frequency has to be delivered to the target at a very close proximity to the receiving diaphragm.'

'Receiving diaphragm?' Palmer asked, seeking clarity.

'The ear,' Layne explained.

'So delivery by phone would be just perfect,' Palmer went on, his brain now racing.

'Yes sir,' Randall nodded. 'And it would seem that that's what he was showing you in the case of the Mayor's secretary – an example of his power. The other fatalities so far would have been caused by him calling a number at random.'

A thought occurred to Palmer.

'How do *you* know we are investigating these cases? The media don't know the victims are linked, or how they were killed, and we haven't released any information on weapon or method. So how come you've got all this information?'

Commander Layne took the question and gave the stock evasive answer.

'That's above our pay scale, Justin.'

Gheeta knew how they knew. She'd always been open with Mark and had discussed this case with him as she had other cases previously. How could she tell Palmer that she was living with a Naval Secret Service operative, and didn't even know it? All those evasive answers he had given her whenever she had asked about his work made sense now. She knew he worked at the Navy Desk in the Ministry but assumed it was a normal Civil Service position, not an intelligence agency position. Christ she felt stupid! She kept her head down and avoided eye contact with Mark.

Palmer thought for a moment and turned to her.

'Sergeant, get Claire to find the last calls received on each of the victims' mobiles. They would have been from North.'

Things were starting to make sense to Palmer now.

'So George North did a bunk with his little piece of equipment and decided to make it pay. But why?'

'The politics changed, sir,' Randall explained. 'To develop a delivery system that could deliver the required frequency strength to just a small two-storey building from any distance would need a development budget starting around a hundred million, and that's a conservative estimate. The problems would be enormous, and the technology completely new; it would be comparable to NASA putting the first man on the moon. The time factor alone would be forty years plus, so the decision was taken to mothball it.'

Palmer nodded. He was beginning to understand this man North.

'And presumably mothball North as well?'

'Early retirement, sir. He took it, but he didn't like it.'

'I can empathise with that.'

'Me too,' the Commander added.

Palmer thought for a moment.

'Okay, so where are we now? North just took off one day, did he – just like that – and disappeared? Spur of the moment decision?'

Randall smiled.

'No sir, George North planned this. He planned it well in advance. He left the service and for a year did consultancy work for the big telecom companies; he kept his head down. We monitored him closely for six months, as we do with all senior staff with privileged information that leave or retire. It's normal procedure, nothing out of the ordinary. Then six months ago he took a holiday in Germany and vanished; until now.'

Sergeant Singh spoke.

'How did he get the weapon?'

Randall was embarrassed.

'He either took it with him when he left, or got it out bit by bit over a period of time before he finally left. It's only a small box, the size of a cigarette packet.'

'Well,' Palmer said, taking a deep breath. 'We have got a bit of a situation on our hands then haven't we, eh?'

The Commander rubbed his chin.

'I suggest Randall works with your team, Justin. He has all the information and files on North and the technology involved. Anything else you want just ask me.'

'North's present whereabouts might help.'

'That we can't help you with I'm afraid. Not that we don't want to, we just have no bloody idea.'

****

Chapter 8

Gheeta was furious.

'I nearly died on the spot, Mark. I could not believe it was you!'

Singh had arrived back at her apartment, after checking in with Claire and calling it a day. Mark was already there. He sat on the lounge window seat as she took her shoes and uniform off in the bedroom, the anger in her voice resonating around the apartment. He laughed.

'Fancy both of us working on the same case, eh?'

Gheeta came through from the bedroom in sloppy jumper and jeans.

'Never mind that. Who the hell are you, Mark Randall? Who am I sharing my life with? I meet you at a security conference, you tell me you work in security for the armed forces, and I naturally think you're military police.'

'I am, sort of.'

Randall was trying to make light of his subterfuge, but Gheeta was not having it.

'Military police don't work in the advanced weaponry field, Mark. Don't treat me like a fool, okay? Military police aren't on first name terms with Defence Ministry Naval Commanders. What are you, Six or Five?'

'Pardon?'

'You. Ae you MI6 or MI5? I'd guess Six.'

Mark rose and looked out over the Thames, avoiding Gheeta's angry look.

'You'd guess right with Six. Look Gheeta, I'm sorry. You know what it's like. What you don't know can't hurt you.'

She took no notice.

'And where did MI6 find you? You don't apply for that kind of job, they find you. Where did they find you, Mark? What is your past?'

'N14.'

Gheeta was getting even more angry.

'Jesus, Mark! N14 is the lot that get the SAS out of trouble when they muck things up!'

Mark laughed.

'Well I never had to do that.'

Gheeta wasn't laughing.

'I need time to think this through. You've not been honest with me. You've used information I've given you; that's the only way your Commander would know Palmer was involved in this case. You should have told me you were involved with North as soon as I talked about the murders. You knew all the time he was doing it and said nothing to me, nothing. And if you are N14, then you will be on the watch lists of Iran, Iraq, and any other country we are in conflict with. Christ, Mark! I could be associated with you, and probably have been. I could be on those lists now too! Being watched, files raised about me and my family! Fuck you, Mark Randall! Fuck you!'

She turned and went back into the bedroom, slamming the door behind her.

****

Chapter 9

Palmer stood in his shirt sleeves at his office window, gazing down at the busy evening theatre crowds and tourists as they window-shopped Victoria Street, and took photos of each other beside the revolving Scotland Yard sign. His mind was miles away. Claire's results from the mobile phone companies had been just as he had expected; each victim's last incoming call was from the same unregistered mobile. Yes, they could give him the number of the phone, but he knew full well he'd never find it after what Gheeta had told him about proxy servers. Cul-de-sacs; this case was full of them, and it was full of them because the killer was using technology he knew backwards and bending it to his advantage all the time. The SIM cards, the proxy servers, and the mouse traps; this whole damn internet and mobile phone thing was going to give the criminals of the world a new dawn, a whole new landscape of unregulated criminal opportunities to exploit. He was thankful he had got Sergeant Singh on board; he could use ten more like her.

He sat at his desk and did his customary thing of leaning the chair onto its back legs and against the wall as he swung his legs up onto the desk.

So, Mr George North, you're going to kill a thousand people are you? And just how do you propose to do that, eh? Ring them all up and...

Palmer's body froze

Yes... yes indeed! That would be the only way he could do it... but how?

He felt the adrenalin pumping through him.

Just how could he do it? How could he phone one thousand people at the same time? He'd have to use the mobile network somehow.

He reached for his phone.

****

Sergeant Singh was still angry, very angry; so angry she was shaking a little, and she felt like punching Mark, not a sensible thing to do with a N14 man. She felt that she'd been used, and she had never felt like that before; her defences had been breached by love. Was it love? If it was, it had turned very quickly into anger. Why couldn't Mark have told her the truth about his job? Didn't he trust her enough? She had trusted him. That was a big mistake. They sat in silence in her kitchen, picking at a pizza she'd had delivered; she wasn't in the mood for cooking. The silence needed to be broken by one or the other of them. Her mobile rang. It was Palmer.

'How would he phone a thousand people at once?'

'What, guv?'

Her voice was still a little shaky with anger.

'You all right? You sound out of breath.'

'I'm fine, guv. Just had a jog.'

'I should take it slower Sergeant, if that's what it does to you. Anyway, this North chap has got to phone a thousand people at the same time to put the ultra sound whatsit down the phone to them, hasn't he; so how does he do that? How does he ring a thousand people at the same time?'

'I don't know, guv.'

'He'd have to use a network, wouldn't he? Key into it and get it to do the ringing out. So how would he do that?'

'I don't know, guv. I'll find out first thing in the morning.'

'Okay, get that Randall bloke to help you. But don't give away too much – I don't trust him. See you in the morning. Goodnight, Sergeant.'

'Goodnight, guv.'

She flicked the phone off. Palmer's words, *'I don't trust him'*, bounced around her head; Palmer was very rarely wrong in character assessment. She looked Mark straight in the eye, her mind made up.

'Tonight you are on the sofa. Tomorrow you're out of my life. No 'ifs', no 'buts'. I want you out of here tomorrow. We will work together on this case in a professional way only. Our personal relationship is ended here and now.'

And she went back into the bedroom, shutting the door and slipping the catch on behind her as tears welled up.

****

Chapter 10

He glanced at his watch; half past midnight, not too bad. He stepped over his dog Daisy, who raised a lazy eye and wished he'd hurry up and go to bed so she could jump up onto the sofa, which she was banned from for a comfy night. Mrs P. was already in bed so the coast was clear if Palmer forgot to shut her in the hall.

'Know anything about mobile phones do you, Daisy?'

The dog recognised its name, but the rest was gibberish.

'No, don't suppose you do. Mind you, very high ultra frequency is more your line, eh? You dogs hear things we humans can't, don't you eh? A different world; amazing.'

Palmer had long since understood that the human race knew very little about what was really going on in the natural world around it, and on a 24-hour time scale of evolution humanity had barely passed the one minute mark.

He went down the hall and into the kitchen for his usual glass of milk before bed, his mind tossing and turning the facts of the case like a mad washing machine. Nothing was clicking together, none of the jigsaw pieces were fitting together yet. He'd read North's security file, and he seemed an ordinary bloke with no hang-ups: well-paid, bit of a loner, but many scientific types are, it goes with the job. Bit like a copper, a twenty-four hour thing; your mind never leaves the office although you do.

Palmer drained his glass and washed it before starting up the stairs. Daisy was up into the lounge and settled on the banned sofa before he'd reached stair three. But just how was North going to kill these people – a thousand of them? He had thought that Sergeant Singh would have known, or at least had an idea of how it could be done with all her IT knowledge, and he had been quite surprised when she hadn't. Even he knew that cold-calling companies could dial out hundreds of numbers at once and talk to the first one who picked up. She hadn't seemed herself on the phone.

He had a quick wash in the bathroom, cleaned his teeth and quietly entered the dim bedroom; Mrs P.'s shape took up her half of the bed. He hoped Sergeant Singh and that Randall bloke got some answers from the mobile networks in the morning. That had to be the key…

He stopped in his tracks, his shirt half off. Of course it was! A smile spread across his face. Of course it was – delivery… What had the

Commander said? They'd shut down North's research because the technology required to *deliver* the weapon would take forty years to develop. No it wouldn't, Harry my old mate, no it jolly well wouldn't – bloody North had worked it out already, and was about to prove it! Fuck!

The expletive left his lips by mistake. Mrs P. stirred.

'I suppose that language means you've been with Professor Latin today? He's a bad influence on you.'

****

Chapter 11

'Through a mast. He's going to get the signal to his victims through a mast.'

Palmer looked up from his desk and the reams of paperwork he kept meaning to make a start on. Singh and Randall had entered his office and stood like errand boys returning with the goods. Singh motioned Randall to a spare chair and sat behind her desk, lowering the laptop from her shoulder as she spoke.

'We've been to all three major players in the mobile network field and each one says the same. You have two methods of delivering a message to that number of people; one, all their numbers would have to be fed into a computer programme which can then ring them all at the same time and relay the message; or two, you hot-wire into the circuit at the point of delivery, which is a telecoms mast, and deliver the message from the mast to the company server, which then forwards it individually in a split second to all the mobiles that mast serves. Or you can pick and choose numbers, but that needs a lot of time programming at the server end, and North wouldn't have the time or the access. He is going to hot-wire his little box of tricks to a mast.'

Palmer took a deep breath.

'Which means that if my or your mobiles were on that server, we'd get the call?'

'Yes'.

'Why did North say he'd kill a '*thousand*' people then? That's a specific number.'

'It's a ball park number, sir,' Randall explained. 'But he's well, well out. The current estimate of the number of mobiles on a mast server is approximately eighty thousand, and each of the three major services comes up with that same figure.'

'So if each mast is transmitting through its servers to about eighty thousand phones, and there are three main networks tied into that mast's server, then it's transmitting to about a quarter of a million phones at any given time?'

'Yes.'

'How many masts are there in London?'

'Well, depends on what you call London; but let's take it as within the M40 motorway ring… fourteen thousand.'

'Fourteen thousand masts, and North could choose any of them to wire in his little box of tricks?'

Randall nodded.

'We can't possibly physically monitor all those masts, guv.'

Singh cupped her head in her hands.

'We would need fourteen thousand bodies!'

Palmer thought for a moment.

'So we have to whittle it down then, don't we – to probabilities and possibilities. Any ideas?'

Randall took his jacket offm as civil servants tend to do to give a false impression of starting work, and hung it over Palmer's on the coat stand, which didn't go down to well.

'We have a clue, sir. North took consultancy jobs at three mobile companies when he left the service; but only one of those was a service provider. The other two were research companies working on circuit boards and internet viabilities.'

Palmer moaned inside at the word 'internet'; some more opportunities for the criminal world, no doubt.

'Which service provider was it?'

'GT, Global Transmitters.'

Palmer leant his chair back against the wall and swung his feet onto the paper mound on his desk.

'So, an educated guess at this stage would assume North will use the GT signal to send his deadly call and kill enough people to scare the Mayor into paying the ransom. So he's going to somehow intercept the signal at a mast and push out his signal. How difficult is that?'

'Very simple, guv. Sorry.'

Singh smiled apologetically.

'Would be, wouldn't it.'

'It's all fibre optic cables,' Sergeant Singh explained. 'Each one is thinner than a hair, and each one can carry up to ten thousand phone conversations. So, all he has to do is open the box of tricks at the foot of the mast, and divert the cable through his box of death and hey presto, he's in. And, it's the same technology for all three major mobile networks, so he could wire into all three at once.'

'Christ, he's certainly got the upper hand hasn't he, eh? Any luck on tracing him yet?'

Randall shrugged.

'None, sir. Every lead goes stone dead after he went to Germany.'

'Got it all planned hadn't he, eh? No loose ends. The clever sod.'

The office phone rang. Sergeant Singh took the call.

'It's the Mayor, guv. For you.'

Palmer took the call on his line.

'Mr Mayor, what can I do for you?... Who?... Have they?... Have they indeed?... Yes, yes… Say about an hour, okay?... Right.'

He put the phone down and sat thoughtfully for a moment.

'Well, we have underestimated Mr George North haven't we, eh?'

Randall shifted uneasily.

'Underestimated how?'

Palmer took a deep breath.

'Our friend the Mayor has had the MDs of all three major mobile phone networks on the line to him. Each one has had a ten million pound ransom demand, and each has been told to refer to the Mayor's office for details.'

****

The Mayor's office was very quiet. Palmer finished explaining the situation to the three astonished mobile phone network MDs and sat back.

'So you see, gentlemen, he can do what he says; he's proved that. And by doing it he not only kills roughly a quarter of a million innocent customers of yours, but as I am sure you have already realised, puts you out of business.'

The Mayor frowned.

'How?'

Palmer eyed him seriously.

'Have you answered a mobile phone call since the other day?'

'Not likely!'

'Exactly, and nor will anybody else once this whole thing goes public. Nobody will want to know about mobile phones, let alone use them.'

'We'd be finished overnight,' the Celcall MD said.

'Pay him off. We have to pay him off,' said Mr Premier Network, sounding very worried.

'And then what?' said Mr Global Transmitters, in a state of near panic. 'He'll still have the means to do it!'

Sergeant Singh had been watching. She caught Palmer's eye.

'May I say something, sir?'

'Of course, go ahead.'

Singh looked from one to the other of the MDs.

'How easy is it to close your networks down? And by that I mean keep the mast transmitters live, but block any calls from coming into them.'

Silence greeted this for a moment.

'Close down?'

Mr Celcall saw his company's revenue stream stopped in its tracks.

'Why close it down? North will just wait until we start up again and then do it.'

Singh smiled.

'Okay, just let me run this past you. Let's say North says he's going to make the calls at midday; so, at 11.59, by which time he's got his little box of tricks in position and ready, you shut the incoming call circuits down. He won't know the circuits are dead, and when he makes his call he will be the only person making a call in the London area. His UHF transmitter has to be powerful enough for us to be able to pick him up on cross-positioned scanners, and pinpoint him by marking his signal from two different positions.'

'It could work. The theory is sound,' said Mr Top Phone, sounding impressed.

Palmer saw a plan forming.

'So, can you gentlemen arrange for a total shutdown of your incoming call systems without it going public in advance? We need Mr North out there with his signal so we can nab him.'

'If we want a business left afterwards we have to, Chief Inspector.'

The Celcall MD was still counting beans. Palmer nodded.

'It's Chief Superintendent. Good, then my Sergeant will be your contact point. When she says 'cut', you cut.'

Gheeta smiled benevolently at the three MDs. She addressed the Global Transmitters MD.

'I need a meeting with your server engineers, as our man is on your network. I've an idea that may be of use, but I need to work it through. Can we arrange that?'

'Of course, anytime you like.'

Global Transmitters MD was grabbing at any straw.

****

Chapter 12

George North looked down from his sixth-floor hotel room window onto London's busy Park Lane traffic. A smile of self appreciation crossed his face. Forty million pounds; a nice thought, that, a very nice thought indeed.

He checked the BBC News Channel on the hotel TV, and then MSN news on his laptop; still nothing in their bulletins about the Mayor being killed. North would have loved to have been there when he took the call on his mobile. Probably the police had put an embargo on the story; can't frighten the population by telling them their Mayor had been murdered by a phone call. He laughed out loud. Forty million; yes, a very, very nice thought.

He picked up his passport from the bedside table. Ahfed Garranchi, Diplomatic Attaché, Italian Embassy, Peru; amazing what money can buy.

Two floors above him on the hotel roof, a mobile phone mast stood grey against the sky, buzzing softly as it facilitated ten thousand calls every second. In four days' time, if no money was paid, it would become a Weapon of Mass Destruction.

****

Chapter 13

'It looks like it's got the measles.'

Palmer stood in the team room with Randall, looking at a map Sergeant Singh had spread out on a table. It was a map of London's mobile phone masts, and she had inked the M25 in green as a border, and within that circle was a mass of red dots, each one being a telecoms mast.

'I hope all those signals in the air really can't have an effect on the human brain, guv. What with radio and telecoms and satellites and the rest of the signals buzzing around out there, think of all that going through your head every second of the day!'

Palmer smiled.

'Yes, and you still can't find a programme worth watching on a Friday night can you, eh?'

Randall leaned over the map.

'So where do we start? Needle in a haystack is an understatement looking at this lot.'

'You two start with this.'

Palmer picked up a spiral bound engineer's reference book and handed it to Randall.

'This is a full list of all the aerials and where they are. See if we can discount any because of their position or access; for instance, if an engineer needs a forty- foot ladder or hoists to get up to the mast, cross it off the list. It won't get rid of many, but any that we can find to whittle the number down is a bonus. North will have sorted his mast out by now, and it's going to be one with easy access and a reasonably secure location where he can do his work unnoticed. Chop chop then, let's go. Get on with it.'

'Guv, take a peep at this.'

Palmer had forgotten about Claire, working away at her keyboard in the corner. She turned in her chair and smiled excitedly.

'I think I've got an address for Mr North.'

Palmer crossed quickly at that remark and pulled a chair up beside her.

'Go on.'

'Well, just routine really. I input George North into the Land Registry database.'

'The what Registry?'

'Land Registry, it's a national database where the owners of every bit of land and property in the UK are listed. If you buy or sell a house your solicitor has to check with them to make sure you own it, and then update the files to the new owner's name.'

'Right.'

'Anyway, there's loads of George Norths, as you might imagine.'

'Is it legal for you to access the Land Registry database?'

Palmer wasn't unduly worried whether it was or was not; he was just curious. He knew there were many databases that Sergeant Singh had hacked into and set up secret lines of communication with that were classified and password protected – or so their owners thought. Banks, building societies and credit card companies for a start. She'd won a bet with him by having his credit card details and spending record for the past year up on a screen within three minutes.

He turned to face Singh, who had heard the question. She smiled and nodded.

'That one is perfectly legal, sir.'

'Okay Claire, go on.'

'Well, checking with North's employment record he has lived in a company provided house or apartment for the past sixteen years, so I shifted the search down to the time prior to that. Another point is that he's a bachelor boy; most owners are husband and wife, so I restricted the search further to a single name owner. There were still quite a few George Norths, though – so what about middle names? He hasn't got one; bit unusual, but that got the list down to just sixteen.'

She pressed a key and the printer whirred.

'And hey presto, there they are.'

She whipped the printed sheet off and handed it to Palmer. He beamed at it like a kid in a sweetshop with ten pounds to spend.

'That is good, well done Claire. Right then, let's get these out to the local boys and see what we can find.'

Three o-clock in the morning parked in a West Norwood side street was not Palmer's idea of heaven; and it was drizzling. He sat in the back of the plain squad car with the local CID chief and a driver in the front. They all looked through the windscreen to a semi-detached house fifty yards up the road.

'I bet he's not in.'

Palmer was tired.

'I'd go with you on that, Justin,' Inspector Mann of South Thames Division CID agreed. 'No movement in or out all evening, and no lights going on or off. Bloody place is empty.'

The offside car door opened and Sergeant Singh slipped quietly in and smiled at Palmer.

'Good morning, Sergeant. Sleep well?'

Palmer was being sarcastic. Singh and Randall had been here as long as he had.

Claire's printout had borne fruit, with five addresses that couldn't be discounted from a suspect list due to lack of information on the 'George Norths' that lived at them. Four had proved to be totally innocent homes of somewhat bemused gentlemen, all called George North, for whom a visit from the local police had proved to be a novelty and just a little unnerving, especially being the plainclothes branch. The West Norwood one had proved more interesting. Preliminary enquiries by the local CID had turned up the fact that this George North had asked for no mail deliveries and elected to pick up his mail from a post office box instead. He was a very low-profile person, and a police officer posing as a gas fitter come to service the boiler had got no answer; and after knocking at the neighbours, which was the real reason for the visit, had been told that Mr North had only been seen very occasionally, and never passed the time of day or even acknowledged his neighbours should they be around.

Palmer reached for the car door handle.

'Right then, let's go see what we can find.'

They left the car and were joined by Randall, two uniformed officers and two firearms officers, fully armed. They silently approached the front door through the small paved front garden.

'Not a flower lover, is he?' Palmer commented, observing the concrete.

'I think it's called 'low maintenance' these days, guv,' said Sergeant Singh.

Palmer stopped Inspector Mann's hand just as he was about to push the front doorbell.

'I'd rather he didn't know we are here, Geoff; rather take him by surprise. And it's odds on he's not going to be in there anyway.'

Randall leant forward and whispered to Palmer.

'I'll go round the back, sir; in case he does a runner that way.'

He nodded to Randall and gave him a minute to get round the back, before indicating to the uniform officer to be ready to use the handheld door ram. Inspector Geoff Mann smiled; he had worked with Palmer before and was used to his circumvention of the rules when it suited.

'Left the warrant in the car have you, Justin?'

Palmer felt his pockets hurriedly. A feigned look of shook crossed his face.

'Do you know, Harry? I believe I have! Oh well, get it later eh?'

He nodded for the door ram to be used. 1930s wooden doors don't take a lot of smashing to open them, and one swipe with the ram on the lock was enough. The wood splintered around it and the door swung invitingly open.

'Careful!'

Palmer held back Gheeta, who was about to rush inside.

'This guy's clever; could be booby traps. After you, gentlemen.'

The firearms officers entered slowly, weapons at the ready.

****

Chapter 14

George North lay on top of the hotel bed. A pay-per-view video flickered on the television, but his attention was taken from it as one of the two mobile phones on the duvet beside him vibrated. He turned it off and keyed in a number on the second mobile phone, into which he pushed a single jack plug that had its other end connected into a small eight-inch cubed black box. He pressed the call button and listened as the mobile rang out the number. The unmistakeable sounds of a mobile ringing tone came from the small speaker on the side of the cube.

'Come along Mr Plod, answer the phone.'

****

Chapter 15

'Don't answer that unless you want to die!

Palmer barked out the order when the mobile rang. They all looked round at the small Nokia 140 lying on a side table in George North's hall and ringing invitingly, its aerial flashing like a tasty bit of bait. He turned to Sergeant Singh.

'Can we get a trace on that call when it ends?'

Singh shook her head.

'I can take the sim card out and get the number, but trying to trace it will probably just lead us through another mouse trap of proxy servers, sir.'

'He knows we are bloody well *here*.'

Palmer was realising North was a very worthy adversary.

'He's a clever one, isn't he – leading us around and second guessing our movements. Okay, get Forensics in asap and see if they can find anything in the house that could tell us where he is. The bugger knew we were here.'

'He could just be watching from up the road, sir.'

Gheeta thought that was the most likely way North would know when the police were in the house and when to make the call, but Palmer shook his head.

'No, too simple for him. He's a 'planner'; he's got this whole caper planned out to lead us through the hoops, give us little morsels that lead us along and point us in different directions so that he knows exactly what we are doing. We need to upset the plan somehow, so he panics and breaks cover.'

He stifled a yawn and checked his watch.

'Blimey, is that the time? Come on, leave Forensics to do their work. Let's go and get some sleep.'

****

Palmer got dropped off at home by a squad car as dawn was breaking over Dulwich and walked slowly up his front garden path, admiring the flowers and their scent which always seemed stronger to him in the early morning air. Mrs P. looked after the gardens, front and back, and it was her passion: manicured lawns and flower beds planted to give the optimum colour and fragrance all year round. She'd planted a new rose bed in the front garden earlier in the year, and it was a feast of colour and perfume. He stood on tiptoe to smell a white rose called Peace covering the top of the fence between his house and his next door neighbour Mr Benjamin, known to everybody in the neighbourhood as Benji.

Benji was not one of Palmer's favourite people; an ex-advertising executive in his early sixties, with a liking for designer clothes, jewellery, fake tans and '*poncing around like a prat*', as Palmer put it. A new car every year and three expensive holidays, usually 'singles' cruises, to some far-flung exotic island group. For some reason that Palmer couldn't understand, Mrs P. and her lady friends in the WI and Gardening Club thought Benji was wonderful. Bald on top with a ponytail was the icing on the cake as far as Palmer was concerned. He'd said to Mrs P., '*you know what you find under every pony tail don't you, eh? An arsehole.*' She didn't appreciate that and had told him to wash his mouth out.

Although the daughter of a petty South London criminal, Mrs P. had tried to pull herself and Palmer up the social ladder; although in Palmer's case it was snakes and ladders – up one rung, and down three. She had long ago accepted that she wouldn't ever change him, and in her deepest heart she didn't really want to. A rough diamond he was, and a rough diamond he would always be. She was proud of his career, proud of the way they'd brought up their children, and very proud of her house and gardens. It was all a million miles from the small terraced house in Milkwood Road, Loughborough Junction she and her three brothers had been brought up in; the garden there was a twelve-foot square of cracked concrete that was usually piled high with very dubious merchandise her dad had 'found', and a ladder was always propped up against the back wall in case there was a knock on the door early in the morning, and dad had to make a quick exit over the railway marshalling yard behind. The knock on the door and the quick exit was usually when the young DC Palmer came with a warrant; something between them had clicked, and the rest is history. Forty years on, and both continued to surprise the other.

Palmer took another long sniff of the rose. The perfume was exquisite, but through the leaves over the fence what Palmer saw was not.

'What the – ouch!'

He pricked his hand as he pushed the roses apart for a better look. What he had seen was that a rather over-large hot tub had been installed on Benji's front decking and was gently steaming away. Palmer pulled an iron chair from Mrs P.'s front lawn set of four and table and stood on it for a better view. It was indeed a very large hot tub; but then Benji would have to have the biggest and most expensive available, or it wouldn't be Benji.

****

'It's bigger than your kitchen.'

Palmer had come inside, patted the dog, washed and donned his pyjamas in the en-suite bathroom before going into the bedroom. Mrs P. stirred as he took another look out of the window at the hot tub.

'What time is it, Justin?'

'Quarter past five. Have you see that hot tub Benji's had installed? Talk about big, you could book a cruise in the bloody thing!'

Mrs P.'s voice was muffled from under the duvet as she tried to shield her face from the light thrown into the bedroom by Palmer opening the curtain wider to look down at the tub.

'It's very nice, Justin. He's invited the Gardening Club round to christen it next week.'

'What? I hope you are kidding. Are they going to put their costumes on and jump in?'

Mrs P.'s head appeared, her eyes blinking in the light.

'Of course we are. How else would you christen a hot tub? I'm looking forward to it – champagne and buffet, all provided by Benji.'

'You're going?'

'Yes, and you're invited as well.'

'No way, too dodgy that. Some of those Garden Club members are a bit old.'

'So?'

'Well… just thinking about incontinence, that's all.'

'Don't be so vulgar, Justin. Trust you to think of that.'

'And flatulence. Knowing Benji he'll have lots of those silly little floating perfume candles. If you see any bubbles coming up, extinguish all naked flames!'

He laughed. He was enjoying the thought of the Gardening Club members in a hot tub.

'And there's Benji's fake tan too; that might wash off and you'll all get out with a beige tint!' He laughed even more. Mrs P. swung her legs out of bed and stretched.

'Well, thank you for waking me so early. Do you want anything to eat?'

'No, I'm going to catch a couple of hours' sleep and then grab a bar of soap and have a bath in his tub when he's out. Save on our heating won't it, eh? I'll take the dog in with me.'

He was still giggling as Mrs P. gave him a withering look.

'If anything happens to that hot tub, Justin Palmer, you will be first in the frame.'

****

Chapter 16

Palmer exhaled loudly. He was in a small café off Trafalgar Square, sitting opposite Commander Layne. He took a sip from his coffee and cleared his throat.

'Thank you, Harry. Not what I wanted to hear, but I appreciate you keeping me in the loop.'

The Commander shrugged.

'Least I could do, Justin. But you didn't hear it from me, okay? It really is one of those *for your eyes only* things. Upstairs wanted to let it roll on, but I could see trouble ahead with that strategy.'

****

Chapter 17

North's mobile was humming on the hotel bed. He picked it up.

'Yes.'

The voice on the other end was curt.

'You got the Mayor's secretary, not the Mayor.'

'Damn! I wondered why there wasn't anything on the news about it.'

'We need a high-profile victim, George. They won't pay up no matter how many Joe Publics you kill; but one celebrity and the cheque will be in the post right away.'

'Any suggestions?'

'No, but I was thinking… You're in a top hotel; they must get 'names' staying there. Easy to ring their room number and…'

The voice trailed off. North smiled

'Of course. Leave it with me.'

The line clicked off. He crossed the room and looked out of the window, down onto the small drop off and pick up point in front of the hotel, where a queue of five limos and taxis waited for their passengers or were dropping them off.

****

Chapter 18

'Who?'

Palmer raised his eyes from reading George North's CV and looked across the office with an inquisitive expression.

'Jamie Donnello.'

Gheeta felt an explanation was in order, as she knew Palmer's knowledge of the entertainment world could at best be described as nil.

'He is, or he was,' she explained, 'the winner of a television talent show last year. He's just had a number one single and was on a national tour.'

'Jamie Donnello?'

Palmer was none the wiser.

'Yes.'

'Sounds like Spanish for Jammy Dodger.'

He rose from his desk and started to put on his jacket and trilby.

'I take it you're telling me that he's been found dead in his hotel room because the circumstances of his death are similar to our other corpses?'

'Trickle of blood from the ear, guv.'

She said it in a resigned manner, shut her laptop and put it into its shoulder case, before following Palmer out of the office and down the stairs.

'Big name was he?'

'As big as they get these days, guv. All over the teen magazines, signed a big money deal with a record company, plenty of TV exposure, and a million and a half twitter followers.'

'Million and a half twits more like; and he'll be forgotten next year when the next one hit wonder comes along.'

'Yes, guv.'

Gheeta didn't bother to answer him, although she was quite fond of Donnello's songs. She had long suffered Palmer's scathing remarks about TV talent shows and a certain Simon Cowell's fortune made on the back of people's misplaced hopes.

They crossed the foyer and got the duty officers to pull a panda car in to ferry them to the hotel. Palmer relaxed in the back, while Gheeta pulled out her mobile.

'I'd better give Mark Randall a call and he can meet us there if he's free.'

Palmer waved a hand sideways.

'No, don't bother him yet. I saw Commander Layne yesterday and Randall's pursuing another line of enquiry for him. We'll see what's what at the hotel first. I bet we won't be able to keep the media out of this one though, not if the record company sees a few thousand 'sympathy' sales of this bloke's records on the horizon.'

Gheeta shock her head in mock disbelief.

'Guv, only you would think that way.'

He laughed.

'Yes, me and the record company, Sergeant. Give the Yard's PR department a ring and see if we can put out a press release limiting the death to 'unknown causes'. Being a pop star the media will think straight away it's drug related, and they'll be off trying to find links between Mr Dodger and his dealers. That should give us some time.'

'Donnello, guv. Mr Donnello.'

'Didn't I say that?'

'You know you didn't, guv.'

Palmer smiled.

'Have you got a hot tub, Sergeant?'

Gheeta wondered where on earth the conversation was going now. What had a hot tub to do with Donnello's murder?

'I live on the fifth-floor, guv.'

'Hmm.'

Palmer dropped the subject as they pulled up outside the very opulent Majestic Hotel, Park Lane. Palmer was impressed.

'I don't think Donnello's royalties would go very far in this place.'

They left the police car and fought through a melee of press people, helped by the sharp elbows of the commissionaire and Palmer's size elevens 'accidentally' tapping a few ankles on the way. Once inside the manager introduced himself and took them by lift to the third floor and Donnello's suite. The West End Central CID was working inside with Forensics. The local Detective Sergeant stepped forward as they entered.

'DS Lydbrook, sir, West End Central.'

Palmer introduced Sergeant Singh and took a look at the body lying beside the bed. The telltale trail of blood from the right ear had dried in place, looking like a narrow scar. He straightened up.

'Okay Sergeant, bring us up to date.'

Lydbrook cleared his throat as though about to deliver a long speech. Palmer anticipated it.

'Short and concise please Sergeant, if you would. Time is of the essence.'

'Well sir, the hotel housemaid found the body when she came in to do the daily clean at about ten this morning. Local doctor was called and pronounced the lad dead, and he called us in as he was suspicious about the blood from the ear and thought it might be drug related.'

'Really?' Palmer said, sounding surprised. 'I thought you shoved charlie up your nose, not in your ear?'

Gheeta had to turn away, stifling a smile. She knew this was Palmer having a kick at present day doctors, most of whom he felt the cash-strapped NHS ferried in from India, with fake diplomas to cover up their shortcomings in training up local people. Lydbrook thankfully ignored the remark and carried on.

'The room's clear; no weapons, no syringe, no pills, nothing. The local beat man called it in to the station, which is when the front desk recognised it fitted your flyer about corpses with blood around the ear. And that's about where we are at, sir.'

Gheeta was looking at the body from all angles.

'Where's his mobile? Has it been bagged?'

Lydbrook shook his head.

'No, nothing's been touched or removed.'

'So he hasn't got one?'

'If he has, we haven't found it yet.'

Palmer was following Gheeta's train of thought; no mobile, so the death call must have come on the landline. He turned to the manager.

'Did you put the phone receiver back on the hook?'

The manager was unaware of the significance of his answer.

'Of course, it was hanging and buzzing.'

Palmer understood why he would have replaced it, not being aware of the phone's part in the murder. He motioned Gheeta to the window out of earshot of the others.

'We have two possible scenarios as I see it; either an outside call coming in, or an in-house call from another hotel room. Could North kill with his machine by putting it through on an internal phone?'

'Yes, it's the sound frequency that's the weapon, and that can be delivered to the ear through the digital chip on any phone. They use the same chips for internal and external phones.'

Palmer was worried.

'Better get down to the hotel switchboard and see if the last call into this room was internal or from outside. If it was internal, then North either came in and made it from a phone in the foyer or lounge or some other public area in the hotel, or he's booked a room. He's upping the ante; he's twisting the Mayor's arm a bit harder by killing a 'name'. I bet he waited for a high-profile victim to check in, probably by sitting in the foyer, noted their room number and bingo! He made the call.'

Gheeta nodded.

'I'll check it; and I'll check the hotel CCTV too, if they've got one.'

Her mobile rang. They looked at each other.

'I'm almost afraid to answer it.'

The screen showed it was Claire calling.

'It's okay it's Claire.'

She took the call, while Palmer wandered back over to the manager who was visibly shocked.

'My Sergeant is going to check your phone records and see who rang Mr Donnello from outside and inside the hotel,' he said, and smiled one of his reassuring smiles at the manager. 'Don't worry, it's just normal procedure. By the way, how did the press get on this story so fast? We had to fight our way through them to get in.'

The manager replied in a shaky voice.

'Probably from one of our staff, Superintendent. I'm afraid we get a lot of celebrities staying here; to be honest I don't agree with it, but the policy is to offer the big agencies a very good deal so we get their 'name' clients. It's good for business, but the downside is that the tabloids and celebrity magazines will offer staff a good cash incentive to leak any tasty stories.'

'It's Chief Superintendent. What are tasty stories?'

'Oh, sorry. You know the type – who's visiting who and staying all night, that sort of thing.'

'Oh, I see.'

He noticed Sergeant Singh beckoning him back.

'Excuse me a moment,' he said, and crossed over to her.

'The Mayor's office has had another call,' Gheeta said quietly. 'Donnello's name was given and the money has gone up a million, with the threat of further big name victims to come if it isn't paid. The Mayor's got the jitters and wants to pay, and the Yard's press office are fielding calls from just about every media company in England about Donnello's 'mysterious' death, and the rumours about a serial killer on the loose in London.'

'Oh shit!'

Palmer took a big breath.

'It's North; he's breaking the story so the Mayor panics and pays.'

Palmer thought for a few moments.

'I'll go and have a word with the Mayor; we need him to stall for a while. I'll get him to give the impression he's going to pay up, and that it will take a little time – red tape, Treasury blocking it or some such excuse. Should give us some precious time.'

Gheeta nodded.

'I'll go and check the phone calls and CCTV. I think I'd better take the manager with me and get him a strong cup of tea; he looks like he's about to collapse into a quivering wreck.'

Palmer cast a glance the manager's way.

'I think he's probably more worried that the only phone calls he's going to get are room cancellations. Can't see anybody wanting to book in here now, can you? Tomorrows headlines should just about kill his business – "Murder at the Majestic!" Read all about it!'

Gheeta smiled.

'I'll see if the doctor's got a sedative I can slip in his tea.'

****

Chapter 19

'Peru?'

It was the next morning, and the Serial Murder Squad team room was buzzing. Palmer's officers were sifting through anything they could find on North and going out in pairs to check it; it was a hard task, as this man was a loner with a high security ID, and was positioned a long way beneath the radar. But, as usual, 'JCB' Claire had managed to dig up one surprising fact for the team.

Palmer repeated the word.

'Peru? He's been to Peru four times in the last six months? Are you sure?'

Claire nodded.

'Positive'

Sergeant Singh entered with a hand full of papers and photos. They exchanged pleasantries.

'Claire reckons North has visited Peru a few times lately.'

'Has he?' Gheeta asked Claire.

'Four times.'

Palmer was inquisitive.

'How do you know?'

Claire threw a 'shall I tell him?' look at Gheeta. Palmer understood that look.

'Oh, I see – one of Sergeant Singh's little programmes, eh?'

He was well aware that Singh had hacked into just about every database and government department back office system that the team could ever want to glean information from, whether they had restricted access or not.

'Border Control Main Frame database, sir,' Gheeta explained. 'It lists all UK incoming and outgoing people from their passport numbers. Government uses it to massage the immigration figures. What they do is –'

Palmer cut her short.

'I don't want to know. I take it we are not supposed to have access to it?'

Gheeta struck an over-the-top innocent expression.

'I couldn't possibly comment, sir.'

'Okay, carry on Claire. What have you got?'

Claire smiled at Gheeta and continued.

'North has flown out to Peru from four different UK airports, which was a bit silly really because if he did that to try and hide the flights it had the opposite effect, because it was his name making unusual detours to get to Peru that flagged him up. Each time he's been there just a few days and then come back.'

‘Well,’ Palmer said, raising his eyebrows. ‘So that’s where our serial killer is making his nest, eh? Get Interpol in Peru to see if they can quietly see what he’s been up to; I’ll lay money that he’s bought a place and set up a bank account in one of those ‘ask no questions’ banks. And put a ‘person of interest’ flag on his passport with Border Control – if he tries to leave the UK they are to detain him and notify us immediately.’

‘There is one other thing, sir. He’s got a flight booked from Heathrow next Thursday.’

‘Oh Christ! So that means he thinks he’s going to have the money wired out and everything settled by then.’

Palmer rubbed his chin thoughtfully.

‘Sir,’ Gheeta said, sounding worried. ‘If he’s not paid off by then, he’s going to try the big kill.’

Palmer nodded.

‘You bet he will; and if he gets an idea that the Mayor is stalling he’s likely, probably more than likely, to arrange more demonstrations of his little box’s power.’

‘We do have one glimmer of hope, sir.’

She looked at one of the papers she was carrying.

'The call made to Donnello was an internal one from the hotel lobby. It's not much, but it's something.'

Palmer shrugged.

'So, either North was staying there, or came off the street to make the call; the only way he'd know Donnello's room number was if he overheard it at reception, or followed him up to the room.'

'He followed him up in the lift.'

'How do you know?'

She passed a clutch of photo prints over to Palmer.

'Prints of stills taken off the hotel CCTV. They show North getting into the same lift as Donnello and his agent and getting out on the same floor, then walking a few yards behind the pair of them as they went to his room. He's then picked up on the foyer camera sitting reading a paper until the agent left and then he goes out of shot, presumably to make the killer call.'

'I reckon he was staying there, you know,' Palmer said, leafing through the stills. 'I can't see the hotel staff not picking up on a bloke who's not a guest or resident wandering around, going up and down in the lift, and sitting in the foyer. Security in a posh hotel like that would be all over him in no time.'

Gheeta took the stills back and put them into her shoulder bag.

'I'll get over there and show these around, see if anybody recognises him. It could be he's still there. That'd make our job easier wouldn't it, eh?'

Palmer waved a finger at her.

'Well, if he is don't do anything silly. Get back to me. I'm going to go see the Mayor again and keep him under control; make sure he plays ball.'

****

The Mayor didn't want to play ball.

'Justin, I've had my secretary killed when it could easily have been me; three of my constituents are dead, and now a pop singer is dead – and all for the sake of a few million quid. The media are onto it, and if I don't pay up can you imagine what will happen if he did manage to kill a few thousand? Can you? Pandemonium, Justin; and one head on the block… mine.'

Palmer nodded sympathetically.

'I fully understand that, Mr. Mayor; I'm not saying don't pay him. Although if you do, as I've said before, what's to stop him coming back for more at a later date?'

The Mayor laughed.

'I would have thought eleven million from me and ten million from each of the three networks would be enough to set him up for life, wouldn't you? I can't see that he'd ever need to come back for more.'

'I'm just covering all the bases. Anyway, I haven't said don't pay him. All I've said is to stall paying him for as long as you can. Believe me, we are getting very close to him now; and with the networks on board with their ability to be able to switch the power off, we can neutralise his actions.'

'Only if you know when and where he's going to send that damn signal out. How will you know that, eh?'

'I don't know that; not yet, anyway. But I do know that as long as he thinks all that cash is coming his way fairly soon, he won't jeopardise *that* pay day. Just stall him – tell him the Council's broke, and you've got to arrange a loan from some Monetary Fund or the Bank of England. Tell him he must understand that you can't tell them what the money is for, as government policy is not to pay ransoms to terrorists – which is what he is, after all – so you're finding it difficult.'

The Mayor let out a long sigh.

'Okay, but one more death because of the stalling, Justin, and I'll pay him.'

Chapter 20

Commander Layne was waiting outside a large solid steel rear gate on a narrow back lane into Gatwick Airport when Palmer's plain squad car pulled up. Palmer lowered his passenger side window as the Commander approached.

'Don't blame us if we are a bit late, Harry. I never knew there were so many little lanes and tracks out here; we've been going up and down them like a ferret up a drain pipe. Sat nav has stopped working, which didn't help.'

'I know, that's us – we block out all communication signals around here except our own. No Sat.Nav. and your phone won't work either.'

Commander Layne smiled and pointed to a dark car pulled up, lights off, further back along the lane.

'We wouldn't let you get lost, Justin. We've been watching you.'

He made a signal and the car moved past them and away. The gates swung open.

'Go through and park on the right by the hangar.'

Palmer's driver edged through the gates, which closed behind them. Palmer noted civilian armed personnel either side in the shadows. His driver pulled the car to a halt beside a long unlit single-storey building. Layne opened Palmer's door; he had a military uniformed person with him.

'Justin, you and I will go inside, and my Corporal will take your driver for some refreshments.'

'I'm okay, sir. Got a flask with me, thank you,' the driver explained.

Palmer leant towards him.

'I don't think that was an offer you can refuse. Better go with the Corporal.'

They left the car and Layne took Palmer through a side door into a very large open plan hangar. But instead of an aeroplane inside which he had expected to see, the place was full of camouflaged tanks and two matt black unmarked helicopters. Layne was aware of Palmer's surprise.

'First law of warfare, Justin – control the skies. And to control the skies, you need control of the airport.'

'Are we at war?'

'No, but being ready for war is the second law.'

They walked around the perimeter of the floor space.

'We have one of these units at every strategic UK airport, Justin. All terribly 'hush-hush', but very useful.'

'Useful?'

'Can't render a hooded and shackled terrorist off to a friendly Arab state for questioning through the public departure lounge can we, eh? If the government needs to get somebody out on the quiet, this is a very secure way of facilitating it.'

'Why you ? You're Navy, not RAF?'

'N14, actually.'

'Say no more,' said Palmer. He knew any questions about N14 wouldn't get an answer.

At the end of the hangar was a guarded lift door. The guard nodded to Layne as they entered the lift; Palmer noted it had four floor buttons, and they were at the fourth floor. Down they went to floor two, and when the door opened and they stepped out it was like entering a modern hotel reception area, the difference being that the staff wore military uniforms and a bank of CCTV screens filled one wall. Layne led Palmer past the desk and down a corridor of what Palmer took to be cell doors. At the end they entered a small viewing gallery, and through the one-way glass Palmer could see

Mark Randall sat at a table, both wrists shackled to it and two guards standing behind him.

Layne pointed through the glass.

'He's not talking. That's the trouble. These chaps are trained to withstand rough interrogation, and of course we can't go down that route; Geneva Convention and all that. No water-boarding allowed here.'

'I'm glad to hear it.'

Layne smiled.

'So, we just fly them out to Saudi or Kuwait and do it there.'

'Do you sleep at night, Harry?'

'I do, but I wouldn't if I didn't have units like this one watching out for us. Think of it that way.'

'I can see your point. Could you do it in a hot tub?'

Layne looked mystified.

'Do what, water-boarding?'

'Sorry, don't know why I said that. Right then, where do we go from here with Mr Randall? We need to find North pretty quickly now; the Mayor's going to stall him, but how long he'll keep that up, and how long North will wait until he realises it's a stall and presses the button is anybody's guess.'

'Right, let me fill you in on Mr Randall. As I told you in our private café meeting, we cottoned onto Randall being in cahoots with North a few weeks ago, and we know he's been feeding North information so that he keeps one step ahead of us. I decided to let Randall run with it, but when you told me about the Peru thing I thought it best to bring him in, as we don't want the pair of them fleeing with the money if it all goes wrong. No extradition treaty with Peru.'

'It won't all go wrong. What's the connection between Randall and North?'

'Randall was North's PO, protection officer, when North was working at Portman Down. People working on new WMDs are targets for other countries that try and get them to jump ship and bring their work with them – and that's not only enemy countries, but friendly ones as well. America is the main culprit; bit like the Premier League in football. A top scientist gets offered a financial package he can't refuse and gets tempted to move; so people like Randall are supposed to keep an eye on their marks and let us know if that is happening. Somewhere along the line this gamekeeper turned poacher and saw that North's ultrasound weapon was a WMD game changer of enormous value and assisted him in smuggling the parts out and then disappearing. Every time we got within touching distance of North, he would be gone. It became pretty clear he was getting inside information, and that pointed at Randall. When you lot became involved after the murders we decided to let you run with it, in the hope that without Randall on your team keeping North up to speed you'd have a good chance of nailing him. Little did we know that Randall was shacked up with your Detective Sergeant and was privy to all your moves as well as ours!'

'I didn't know that either until you told me. I keep my squad's private life away from the office. How did you find that out?'

'I got MI6 to do a deep security check on Randall. Got a shock when it came back with that little bombshell, I can tell you. So that's when I decided to have our little café meet and fill you in.'

Palmer thought for a moment.

'Yes, well I have to admit I tested your theory out when we did a raid on North's West Norwood house. The only way North could have known we were inside and to phone us at that particular time in the morning was if somebody let him know; and the only person who could have done that was Randall, who suggested he go round the back of the house on his own just before we went in. He must have had a prearranged signal that he sent to North. That personal relationship with Sergeant Singh gives me a lever I can use. Shall we get on with it?'

Layne led Palmer out of the viewing gallery, down a few stairs and into the interview room. Randall looked surprised to see Palmer, who sat down opposite him whilst Layne stood away by the door.

'Bit of a bastard aren't you, eh?' Palmer snapped at Randall who looked a bit shocked at the ferocity of the attack. 'Making out you care for Gheeta; moving in, taking all her true affections and giving back your false ones just to get information on North. You're a little shit, Randall. You're not a man, just a two-faced little shit. She still loves you. Won't grass on you. Right now, she's banged up in West End Central. She says she was not working with you, but it's obvious you persuaded her to join you and North in your money-making scheme. She denies it, but it's obvious she's as guilty as you. She gave you the information on what was happening and you passed it to North. No wonder he's always a step ahead of us. Well sorry old son, but neither you nor her are going to get the life of bliss in Peru you had lined up for yourselves; more likely to be Pentonville – a tiny cell in a maximum security wing, locked up for twenty-three hours a day; twenty-four if I had my way. You know, you remind me of the blokes who befriend vulnerable females and steal their life savings; only you stole her heart and her career. CPS reckons the pair of you will go down for assisting murder, and if North manages to do anymore it'll be mass murder. That's life in any judge's book, Randall. Pity… DS Singh was a brilliant detective with a glittering career ahead of her, and a family that loves her – and then you came along and fucked it all up. Nice bloke aren't you, eh?'

Randall spoke in a whisper.

'She's not involved.'

Palmer laughed.

'Bollocks! She's in it up to her neck.'

Randall looked up and spoke loudly.

'She's not. It was just a coincidence she was on the North case; she didn't even know what I did. She thought I was a security consultant. She's nothing to do with it. I should have told her I was on the case, but knowing your moves in advance was a godsend.'

'Wasn't it just! But the only place it's going to send you, old son, is inside – forget Peru. I'll see if we can arrange the two of you to have cells opposite each other, so you can explain to her over the next thirty years or so what a bastard you are. Romantic really isn't it, eh? You'll be able to grow old together – inside.'

Randall shouted with an angry voice.

'She's not fucking part of it, you fool. She had nothing to do with it!'

He was shaking in his shackles; Palmer had him. He leant forward on the table and shouted into Randall's face.

'No, of course not; nothing to do with it. Your living with a key member of the Murder Squad who is after your big mate who is about to share forty million quid with you, and she's nothing to do with it? She's up to her neck in it. What was her share to be then, five million? Bit more than a Detective Sergeant earns, I can tell you.'

He turned away as if to leave, had second thoughts, and returned to put his face into Randall's again.

'Okay, Mr Lover Boy. You know that you are going down for a considerable time, you're not going to Peru or any other place with no extradition ties to the UK, and you're not getting *one* pound, let alone forty million of them. So, if Sergeant Singh is as innocent as you say she is, just tell me where North is; and if we can get to him before his moment of madness, I'll see that the court is told that you assisted us. That might just get the judge to reduce the sentence, so you might get out with a few years of your miserable life left to enjoy in civvy street. And, when we do get North, if he knows nothing about Sergeant Singh, I might be minded to believe she's as innocent as you say.'

He stayed with his face barely twelve inches from Randall's for what, to Layne, seemed an eternity. Randall knew he was in a tunnel with no light at the end, and Palmer had just lit a very small one. His voice dropped to a whisper.

'She has nothing to do with it,' he said, then paused for a moment. 'He's still in the hotel. He's going to wire into the telecoms mast on its roof.'

His head dropped to the desk.

'Tell her I'm so sorry. Tell her I love her.'

'No way,' said Palmer over his shoulder, as he hurried out of the interview room and scuttled along the corridor with Layne trying to keep up. 'Find my driver, Harry. My Sergeant has gone to that bloody hotel with North's mugshot, and if the staff recognise him as a resident she might try and be a hero. She should have more sense, but who knows.'

Layne was confused.

'I thought you said she was in custody? In cahoots with Randall and North?'

'Did I say that, Harry?' he said with a smile at Layne. 'Sometimes I am such a liar. Can't help it.'

Commander Layne despatched one of his men to fetch the driver from the visitor's refreshment room.

'You haven't lost your touch Justin, have you eh? Brilliant strategy that! Mind you, just one thing you got wrong.'

'And what's that?'

They were in the lift going up to ground level.

'He's not going to Pentonville, or any other civilian prison. It will be a closed military court martial and a military prison to follow, probably on an overseas base like Malta. None of this will ever get out – media would have a field day if they thought we'd let a mad scientist with a homemade WMD go AWOL.'

'Well, let's hope we get him before he gets to use it then,' replied Palmer as they exited the lift and ran through the array of tanks and helicopters on the ground floor to the exit. 'Mind you Harry, it is kind of comforting to know this is all here should we need it. Frightening and comforting at the same time.'

Outside they got to Palmer's car as his driver arrived. Palmer winced as he got in.

'Damn sciatica – shouldn't have run just now, gets me now and again. I'll keep you in the loop, Harry.'

They shook hands through the window. Layne was very serious.

'Just remember – when you get him, he's our military prisoner. Let me know, and I'll have him picked up. I could go into that hotel with a team if you prefer, Justin?'

'Oh yes, and that would set the media alight wouldn't it, eh?'

'Just thought I'd offer. You take care old friend, and give my best to Mrs P.'

****

Chapter 21

At the hotel Sergeant Singh was most surprised to find that North was immediately recognised by the manager, and that he was still in residence: Room 88, fourth floor. She tried unsuccessfully several times to get Palmer on his mobile, and even through the control room channel at the Yard, but he couldn't be raised. She decided that being in uniform she'd better keep out of sight, just in case North came down from his room and got spooked by it, so she sat in the manager's office behind reception. A large one-way glass window in the door gave her a good view of the foyer if North should leave. Her mobile rang. It was Palmer.

'Where are you?'

'At the hotel. North is still here, guv.'

'Yes, I know. Don't go near him, there's a firearms unit on its way. Get a side room for them to use to tool up. I've told them to come in one by one, looking like guests. They'll give my name at reception. Okay?'

'Bit like James Bond this, isn't it guv? I'll arrange a room for them.'

'Okay Moneypenny,' he laughed. 'Get through to your network contacts and get the signals from that mast on the hotel roof cut off, that's the one he's going to use. He might have hot-wired into it already so softly, softly is the word. If he gets an inkling we are onto him, he might just press the button.'

'Okay. I've been trying to contact you, have you had your mobile turned off?'

'No, I got into a dead area – I'll fill you in later. I'm on my way – oh, and get a pass key card off the manager so we can get into North's room.'

'Okay.'

She got a pass card and then had the manager label a side lounge as 'Private Meeting'. One by one eight firearms officers arrived, all in civilian clothes and all with the same large suitcase which Singh thought amusing; reminded her of an old Pinewood comedy film with Peter Sellers that her dad used to watch and laugh at. They all gave their name as 'Palmer' and were directed by the Manager to the side lounge. Sergeant Singh waited until they were all present, and then briefed them on the situation with North; all they wanted to know was where he was in the hotel, was he armed, and was he wanted alive? She told them his room and floor, that he was probably armed, but she thought it best not to say armed with a WMD, and she gave them each a printout of his face taken from the lift interior CCTV. Then she rang the networks and had the signal from the roof mast switched off.

Palmer arrived as the evening became dark outside.

‘Right lads, I want to impress on you that this bloke is very dangerous. When, and if, you get him in view, he is likely to try and make a call on a phone, or click a switch, or press a button on some sort of trigger apparatus. We’ve got that covered so let him do that; but he must not be allowed to get away. Understand?’

A chorus of grunts acknowledged the command. Palmer handed the logistics of the operation over to the SFO (Senior Firearms Officer) who sent three through the kitchens and up the staff staircase to the fourth floor where North’s room was; two more went up the main guest staircase where the hotel put a ‘Cleaning in Progress’ sign at the bottom and diverted all guests to the lifts, and another two stayed covering the ground floor and lifts out of view in the manager’s office. Palmer and Gheeta took the lift up with the last one.

****

Chapter 22

North was getting impatient. He checked his watch: quarter past four. Randall should have been in touch by now with an update on the police activity; he guessed the Mayor was probably playing for time on police orders. He should have been out of the country and on his way to a very wealthy life in Peru by now if things had gone to plan. The fly in the ointment was the Mayor. Time to call him one last time, and then if the money wasn't wired out it would be time to show just what he could do. He was angry.

He picked up one of the two mobiles on the hotel telephone table, clipped a voice distorter over the mouthpiece and pressed the Mayor's direct number on speed dial. It rang five times, enough time for the trace equipment in the Mayor's office and the operators to start a trace. North smiled. He'd covered all that by using Eastern European proxy servers and knew the trace would go round and round in circles. The Mayor answered.

'Hello?'

'Where's my money?'

'It's all in hand.'

'It's not in *my* hands. You have thirty minutes to have it wired out to the account I gave you. Thirty minutes.'

'It's the Treasury, they're taking time to put it together. You can't just wire ten million without official sanction. It will be there – just give me a bit more time.'

'Thirty minutes – and it's now eleven million. If it's not done in thirty minutes, say goodbye to a million voters. Your choice. Thirty minutes.'

He clicked off. Time to prove he was not a man to be messed with. The M.O.D. should have realised that when they cut his funding and shelved his project. They thought he was bluffing; well, now they would find out that he wasn't.

He took a suitcase from the wardrobe and delved down to the bottom where his small box of death was hidden. Picking up the two mobiles and putting them and his little box into his jacket pockets, he checked the corridor through the spy hole; all clear. Leaving the room quietly, he hung the 'Do Not Disturb' sign on the door and made his way along to the end of the corridor, and quickly through the staff door onto the staff staircase.

The stairwell wasn't clear. He could hear people coming up from below. Slowly he peered over the rail and down. Hotel staff don't usually wear all blue flak jackets and carry Heckler and Koch MP5SF submachine guns; but the two men two floors down and on their way up did.

North quickly drew back out of sight. His brain raced. He'd obviously been found; but how? Randall? Must be Randall; he hadn't checked in when he should have. He must have been found out somehow. Perhaps Randall talked to save his own skin, otherwise how would the police know he was here? Five minutes more in the hotel room and he'd probably have been caught. North knew he was now on his own.

He kept tight against the staircase wall and went up the flights silently. On the top floor, the seventh, he stopped and listened. No sound from below, and a careful look down showed no activity. Whoever that was coming up, and he guessed it was either a police firearms unit or SAS, had left the staircase; probably left it at his floor to burst into his room.

He pushed open the door to the roof. The cool air and sound of London's traffic hit him. How long had he got? The game was obviously up; he wasn't going to get the money and he probably wasn't going to get away. Okay Mr Mayor, let's see how you explain away the deaths of a few thousand of your electors for the sake of a few million pounds then, eh? See how you like being cast on the scrap heap like I was.

In front of him, bolted securely to the top of the water tower, stood the sturdy thirty-foot steel telecommunications gantry, looking like something from The War of the Worlds, awaiting an order to rip itself from the restraining bolts and attack. The light from tall office buildings around the hotel reflecting from it made it stand out against the dark red sky above. The three major network satellite dishes stood out proud from the sides amongst a host of other smaller discs and antennae.

North smiled. Okay Mr Mayor, okay MOD; let's see who has the last laugh. He started to climb the steel rungs of the water tower ladder.

****

The lift doors opened on the fourth floor and the firearms officer furtively looked out and checked the corridor. At either end his men from the staff staircase knelt on one knee, their weapons ready. He signalled to them and they advanced along the corridor, hugging the walls towards Room 88. Palmer and Gheeta followed behind. Outside the room an officer checked through the spyhole; no movement inside. Gheeta gave him the pass key card, which he silently slipped into the door card reader. He nodded to the other officers, and with a substantial amount of noise they slammed open the door and rushed in shouting: ‘Police!’

The rooms were checked, the cupboards and drawers were checked, the bed mattress was checked; but there was nobody, and nothing to say the room had even been occupied, the only clue a used tea cup.

‘Where the hell is he then?’

Palmer had a sinking feeling. If North had managed to get out of the hotel he could be anywhere; and there was no way of getting to him until he made contact, which he might well do by using his box of tricks.

‘Well, we know he didn’t go down, sir,’ said Gheeta. ‘So he must have gone up.’

They took three armed officers with them and followed in North’s footsteps up the service stairs to the roof door. The officers went through quietly and signalled the all clear for Palmer and Gheeta to follow. Once through onto the roof they waited, crouched in the shadows against the wall, as two officers searched around the roof, checking behind the large air control fan units. They gave the all clear.

Palmer felt a tap on his shoulder. It was Gheeta's hand. He followed the direction of her finger to the mast gantry above the water tower, where the dark figure of North was crouching tight against the base.

'Mr North,' shouted Palmer. 'This is Chief Superintendent Palmer of the Metropolitan Police. Would you come down sir, please?'

There was no reply. He tried again louder.

'Mr North, we've had the phone signals cut off from this mast. Your weapon won't work. The game is over.'

After a short silence North shouted back.

'Do you think isolating this mast will make any difference, Chief Superintendent? There are a hundred of these masts in London, and my signal has the strength to reach quite a few of them from here. You'd better call the Mayor, Chief Superintendent. I want to walk out of here and I want my money. Call him. He's got five minutes left.'

Palmer looked at Gheeta.

'Is that right? Can his signal reach the other masts?'

'Depends on his power source, guv. If the battery in his box is big enough…'

'He's played his trump card then, hasn't he? But he's also signed his own death warrant.'

He turned to the SFO in charge.

'Use the same procedure as for a terrorist with a suicide belt: aim for the head. He's got to go out like a light. Wait for my signal; I'll give a nod. I'm going over to try and distract him. When I see he's not got his finger on the box, I'll give the nod and you take him out, okay?'

The firearms officer nodded and aimed his weapon. Palmer stood ready to walk over to the base of the water tower. Gheeta caught his arm and whispered.

'I have an idea, guv. I talked it through with the engineer at Global Technologies, which is North's mobile network. Keep him talking as long as you can.'

She pressed in a number on her phone and turned out of earshot.

Palmer responded to her request.

'You're not getting any money, Mr North, and you've got two choices of getting out of here. Come down now and walk out in handcuffs, or try and use your little box of tricks and go out in a body bag. There are three sniper rifles trained on you right now.'

'Do you think that worries me, Superintendent? Do you really? If I go then an awful lot of people go with me.'

He held up his box of death.

'I've wired this into the networks; one little press on the switch and thousands of people will answer their phones and die. The networks don't discriminate between people, Superintendent. Could be quite a lot of the rich and powerful in amongst that lot; MPs, royalty, maybe even members of your own family. Think of that, eh? Call the Mayor. He only has three minutes now.'

Palmer was unsure what to do. If the signal was going to be picked up through other masts, then there was nothing he could do. People would die.

'It's *Chief* Superintendent, and I've got the Mayor on the phone right now. He's doing his best. Where is the money to be wired to?'

North was getting angry.

'Stop playing games with me *Chief* Superintendent. The Mayor has all the details. You're just stalling me.'

Gheeta moved close and whispered urgently into Palmer's ear.

'One more call, guv. For God's sake, don't let him press the button yet.'

Palmer had no idea what she was doing as she keyed in another number and turned to be out of sight and earshot of North, but he knew he could trust her one hundred percent to know what she was doing.

'Where's your mate Randall then?'

Palmer didn't want to bring Randall up now, but couldn't think of another way of further stalling North. He noticed Sergeant Singh turn her attention to what he'd just said, and then turn back again to continue on the mobile.

North was silent for a moment. So Randall was still around; the police hadn't got him. Then why hadn't he made contact? Where was he when he was needed?

'Two minutes, Chief Superintendent. Two minutes to Armageddon.'

The firearms officer leant in close to Palmer.

'Shall we take him out, sir?'

Palmer thought quickly.

'No, I can't risk him pressing that button; can't risk him falling on it if you kill him. I'm going over to try and talk to him and try to get him to release the box from his hand. As soon as he does, then you can take him.'

He stood up.

'Mr North, I'm coming over to talk.'

North laughed.

'Oh no, Chief Superintendent, I'm not having any of your funny business thank you. If you come within ten yards of me, I press the button. One minute left.'

Gheeta whispered urgently into Palmer's ear.

'Every mast within forty miles is switched off, his machine is useless now.'

'What?'

Palmer was incredulous.

'Are you sure?'

'Yes guv, no phone in the Greater London area will get his death call except one.'

'One? Which one?'

'The Mayor's. It means North's box will show a green light and he will think all his signals have got through when they haven't. The Mayor won't be answering; I've just spoken to him so don't panic, guv. And then North will get a shock.'

Palmer looked into Sergeant Singh's eyes.

'Is this one of your technical jigsaws that you've got lined up?'

'Yes.'

'Are you sure it will work? There are a lot of people's lives at risk here.'

'It will work, guv. Trust me'

'I always do, Sergeant. Okay.'

He turned to the firearms officers.

'Go get him, lads. No shooting, he can't hurt you now.'

He shouted to North.

'Mr North, we are coming to arrest you now. Your plan has failed.'

North stood up out of the shadows and held his death machine in front of him for all to see. He could see the officers coming for him.

'All right, Chief Superintendent. If you and the Mayor want it to end this way, so be it.'

Theatrically he pressed a button on the machine. His mobile rang. He laughed loudly as he saw the screen indicate it was the Mayor's number.

'Oh my, the Mayor is calling me, I hope he's not ringing to say he's paid the money. Look a bit of a fool now won't he, with a few million of his electorate dead.'

He pressed the answer button and put the phone to his ear.

'Hello Mr Mayor.'

It seemed to Palmer that everything then went into slow motion. North's startled expression lasted for what seemed an eternity, as the phone slid from his hand and he dropped to his knees. The wires tied into the mast pulled his box from his hand as he dropped, and it swung on the end of them like a pendulum clattering against the steel mast with each swing. North's body slid slowly off the mast base onto the water tower, where it rolled to the edge and fell the twenty foot to the hotel roof, landing with a dull thud.

The firearms officers stood with their weapons pointing at the lifeless body as Palmer knelt and turned the head sideways. The line of blood from his ear was still shining in the reflected street light. He turned and looked up at Sergeant Singh.

'Just how did you manage that?'

She smiled.

'Simple. I put 'call divert' on the Mayor's phone to North's phone.'

****

Chapter 23

The late-night revellers of central London crowded round the hotel entrance as North did indeed leave the hotel in a body bag, as Palmer had warned him he would do. In the side lounge Palmer and Singh sat drinking very welcome cups of tea as the firearms team packed away their uniforms and weapons and left.

'So Sergeant,' Palmer said as he moved into a comfortable arm chair. 'Tell me why I shouldn't charge you with murder? You didn't have to use the call diversion from the Mayor's phone. The signals were all cut off.'

'They were, and if his box had registered that his signal wasn't getting through to any mobiles he may well have had an override capacity built in, or even been able to input a repeat function into the network computers so that when they turned the signal back on, bingo. I couldn't take that chance, guv. He was a very clever man; top man in his field. But if even just one signal got through to just one phone, it would register as okay on his box and he'd think it had worked. But that phone would have to be answered by somebody, and who better than North himself? We knew his mobile number from his calls to our three victims and the Mayor's office.'

Palmer thought for a moment or two.

'If the Assistant Commissioner or PCC want answers, I think it might be better to say that North's little box must have malfunctioned.'

Singh smiled.

'Okay, sir. Now, I want you to fill me in on Mark Randall's part in all this. I'm a bit confused.'

'Alright, but you won't like it. Come on, let's get a squad car and I'll drop you off at home. I'll tell you the whole story on the way.'

****

Palmer got out of the squad car in front of his house, thanked the driver and breathed in the cool late-night air. Detective Sergeant Singh hadn't seemed too upset by the subterfuge and double dealing of her now ex-partner; he was pleased about that, as Palmer wasn't one for extending a comforting arm or a shoulder to cry on. Mrs P. had often told him he was devoid of emotions, but the truth be known was that he wasn't, he was just very good at hiding them; a skill developed over many years of police work.

He walked slowly up the drive as the scent from the roses wafted over him. He stood admiring the blooms and stepped into the rose bed, leaning over to smell a few individually; at the same time he wondered why his feet felt wet. Looking down, he saw that his shoes had sunk into the soft earth that was Mrs P.'s prize rose bed, now drowned in a river of water coming under the fence from Benji's garden. On tiptoe Palmer peered over the fence, half knowing what he was going to see; and he wasn't wrong. A half-empty luxury hot tub with a broken side panel was leaking gallons of water across the lawn and under the fence; the wonderful Benji would be getting an earful of Mrs P.'s anger in the morning.

Palmer smiled, looked up towards the heavens, and mouthed the words 'thank you'. It had been a good day, and now it had just got better. He let himself in, quietly giving Daisy a pat in her basket, and took a bottle of cider from the fridge into the lounge, where he settled onto the sofa for a quick five minutes to unwind. Another case put to bed, and pretty soon he would be too.

And then the phone rang.

THE END

The Author

Barry Faulkner was born into a family of petty criminals in Herne Hill, South London and attended the first ever comprehensive school in the UK, William Penn in Peckham and East Dulwich, where he attained no academic qualifications other than GCE 'O' levels in Art and English and a prefect's badge (some say he stole all three!)

His mother had great theatrical aspirations for young Faulkner and pushed him into auditioning for the Morley Academy of Dramatic Art at the Elephant and Castle, where he was accepted but only lasted three months before being asked to leave as no visible talent had surfaced. Mind you, during his time at the Academy he was called to audition for the National Youth Theatre by Trevor Nunn – and forty years later he's still waiting for the call back!

His early writing career was as a copywriter with the advertising agency Erwin Wasey Ruthrauff & Ryan in Paddington, during which time he got lucky with some light entertainment scripts sent to the BBC and Independent Television, and became a script editor and writer on a freelance basis, working on most of the LE shows of the 1980-90s.

During that period, whilst living out of a suitcase in UK hotels for a lot of the time, he filled many notebooks with Palmer case plots, and in 2017 finally found time to start putting them in order and into book form: 13 are finished and published so far, with more to come. He hopes you enjoy reading them as much as he enjoyed writing them.

Keep up to date with Barry Faulkner's new books on his website here;

barry-faulkner.com

You might like to join his reader's club and get advance notice of new books plus free ARCs and other goodies. It's FREE!!

****

Printed in Great Britain
by Amazon

42976132R10079